HIGH RISK

T.S. MAYNARD
W.J. MCNALLY

CHAPTER ONE

THE HIGHER THE CLIMB, THE FURTHER THE FALL. IT'S a cliché that's often overused, but it fit Jim Sloane's predicament perfectly. He clutched a forty-five-degree ledge at the top of a fifty-story skyscraper. His toes dangled over a seven-hundred-foot drop, and an iron fence post, a little over an arm's length in front of his face, dared him to reach for it. The fence was a safety perimeter designed to keep people on the inside of the rooftop, a place Jim desperately wanted to be.

The steep angle and gravity continued to pull Jim down, but his grit and fear kept him plastered to the edge. It was not an exaggeration to say Jim hung by a fingernail. His once pristine Armani suit pants were torn, and his hair whipped back and forth in the frigid Philadelphia air. The fatigue and icy conditions overwhelmed Jim, and his tired eyes pleaded for mercy. He'd been through hell, and he'd almost survived, but almost doesn't count when you're fifty stories high. Just a few more inches and he'd be safe. Finally, he'd be safe.

He pulled his feet over the edge, but his footing was about to give. With his last ounce of strength, he lurched for the iron post, but his hand missed, and he slid backward toward the drop. Death beckoned him closer, and the cliché rang in his head—the higher the climb, the further the fall. For Jim, the fall came on Christmas Day.

As the edge approached, his life didn't flash before his eyes. Instead, his mind filled with thousands, maybe millions, of micro-thoughts that all asked the same question.

How the hell did he end up here?

CHAPTER TWO

FOUR DAYS EARLIER.

Downtown Philadelphia swirled with activity. Folks hurried to complete their Christmas shopping while others toiled at their jobs, eager for the holiday break to begin. The chilly winter weather kept everyone bundled up.

A pair of majestic fifty story skyscrapers adorned with exquisite sculptures on the corners of the roofs overshadowed the rest of the city skyline. The eastern high-rise was more posh than its neighbor and the surrounding area. It was the type of building that had money falling out the windows. One side overlooked the city, and the other faced its lesser twin, separated by an immaculate grass park. Together, the buildings were known as the Banner Towers, and the company that occupied the prestigious top floor of the eastern building was Banner & Brown. This real estate firm dominated the northeastern United States market with plans to take over the world.

On the eve of the holiday break, the bullpen of the office bustled with stressed-out activity. Phones rang, secretaries rushed to answer them, emails were sent, and couriers delivered and took away urgent packages. In contrast to the bullpen's frenetic pace, calm filled the main conference room where ten high-level executives sat in plush black leather chairs around a massive rectangular mahogany table.

Perched at the head, Robert Banner controlled the meeting. A distinguished seventy-year-old captain of industry, he received absolute respect based on his long list of accomplishments, but he also possessed a nurturing quality and was like a stern grandfather from the 1950s. Robert could break out the belt when necessary, or he could sit on the porch and share his wisdom over a glass of lemonade. He spoke in a gravelly baritone voice. "Make sure your secretaries get all the files and supporting documentation together for the SEC inquiry. I don't want any delays or hiccups. Any questions?" Robert waited a moment before moving on to more interesting matters. "Next up, Montgomery Plaza. Sam, what's the status?"

Sam, a short man in his mid-forties with an honest countenance, coughed before addressing the group. "Well, Montgomery Plaza is in a deteriorating neighborhood. Urban blight is inching closer, crime rates are increasing—"

Frank Brown, the sixty-year-old gruff and graying Chief Financial Officer of the company, piped up, "I've got plans for Christmas, Sam."

Sam nodded and regrouped. "Appraised cost is in the fifty to fifty-five million range, but I expect Vanstar to

bid upwards of sixty-million. Based on the most opti-
mistic model in terms of appreciation, rents, and costs,
our rate of return would be fifteen percent in five
years."

"What's your intuition tell you?" Robert asked. He
valued analytics, but he also trusted instincts, a skill
that couldn't be taught with spreadsheets. It was how
the company maintained an edge over its competitors.

"Neither rents nor appreciation will continue
increasing at current rates, especially in this area. Eight
percent seems more realistic. I suggest passing," Sam
said.

Jim Sloane, the sharpest dressed executive in his
pristine Armani suit, shifted in his seat and not so
subtly shook his head.

"Something to add, Jim?" Robert asked.

"Robert, our holdings have dropped twelve percent
over the last three years. We can't keep watching from
the sidelines," Jim said.

Frank leaned forward. "You know the policy, Jim.
Ten percent or it's a no-go."

Jim leaned forward to match Frank's position, a
calculated move he'd learned from countless negotiation
seminars. Matching body language built rapport, and
right now, he needed Frank on his side. "Sam is spot on
with his analysis. Rents will decrease, the building won't
appreciate as fast. We can't control that. We can control
how much we pay. If we get the plaza for fifty million,
we not only hit our goal, we exceed it."

"The market doesn't appear to support that price."
Frank pointed to his copy of Sam's report.

"I can get the price," Jim said.

"How?" Frank asked.

"The same way I got Freemont Hills and the Glassberg building."

Robert leaned back in his chair, clasped his hands together, and placed them under his chin. He glanced at Frank, who showed no emotion. "Sam, strong analysis, excellent work. Jim will take over from here."

It may as well have been a public demotion for Sam, who nodded without making eye contact with anyone. But Jim didn't care. Victory was his. Plus, he wasn't looking to upstage Sam. He couldn't let the company miss out on this golden opportunity. Places like Montgomery Plaza didn't come on the market often.

After the meeting, Jim strutted back to his office. He passed his overweight and high strung secretary, Sharon, who was busy manipulating a spreadsheet on the computer while sipping a giant mug of coffee and nibbling on a blueberry muffin. A career secretary, Sharon's frazzled hair matched her demeanor. Her desk was a clutter of post-it notes, files, and papers.

"Messages," Jim said.

Sharon stashed the muffin and rummaged through a pile of papers until she found the call sheet. "Your wife called at 9:45. She wanted to know what time you'd be—"

"Next," Jim said.

"Your broker called at 10:00 with some good news, and your masseuse called to reschedule your massage."

Jim muttered under his breath, "Guess some people don't want to work." He pointed to Sharon. "Call around, find another masseuse for today."

From across the bullpen, Sam watched the exchange and shook his head.

"Jim, people are leaving for the holidays. I don't think—," Sharon said.

"So don't. Just do it," Jim said. "There must be at least one Jewish or atheist masseuse in the city. Also, get Sam's files on Montgomery Plaza." He scanned her cubicle. "And clean up your desk."

Sharon nodded with gritted teeth as Jim entered his office. Sam drifted over to console her.

Jim paused and took a half-guilty glance at Sharon. Sometimes he expected others to work as hard as him, even though their salaries were a pittance in comparison. He shook off the moment of weakness and shut the massive oak doors to his lavish workspace that included an Italian leather sofa, original artwork, a mahogany desk, a credenza, a washroom with a toilet and sink, and Brazilian cherry wood paneling. No expense had been spared. It was everything an executive defining himself by wealth needed in an office. The only token that acknowledged the holiday season was a small Christmas tree stationed in the corner underneath a painting of the Banner Towers. The plastic replica of a Douglas fir seemed out of place in this miniature palace dedicated to work and money, as did the one solitary personal effect on Jim's desk—a picture of his wife in a sundress standing with their two kids, dressed in Little League uniforms.

Jim settled in his soft leather chair and glanced out the window that featured a view of the western tower and overlooked the pristine park. The phone rang. Jim eyed it, and it rang a second time. He didn't like prospective clients to wait until a third ring. Fortunately, the ringing stopped. Jim waited until the intercom crackled to life.

"It's your wife," Sharon said.

Jim shook his head, picked up, and offered a curt, "Hey."

Maggie cradled the phone against her ear while she opened the day's mail on a simple wooden kitchen table. Her modest view consisted of a small grass backyard peppered with few pine trees, but it also included something priceless—their two boys, aged four and six. The siblings laughed and joked with each other as they passed a soccer ball back and forth in the crisp winter air. A warm soul, Maggie's face had been slightly worn, either by time or the strain of her relationship with Jim. After ten years of marriage, Jim and Maggie had reached a crossroads. Each wanted a life so different from the other. "Thanks for squeezing me in," she said, irritated.

"You know how busy I am," Jim replied.

"Yeah, *I* know. So, when will you get here? The boys have been asking." Maggie ripped open an envelope and pulled out a letter with a header that read, *"Premium Life Insurance - Jim Sloane."*

"I just got assigned a new project, so I can't leave early. I'll catch the eight o'clock flight, which will put me in around ten."

Maggie shoved the mail aside. "Jim, you know they'll be asleep by then."

"Then I guess I'll see them first thing tomorrow. If you hadn't moved so damn far, I could see them tonight."

"They've seen you more since the separation. You actually have to make an effort."

Jim fell silent. The truth stung.

"I'm sorry," Maggie said. "They miss you, that's all."

"And you?" Jim asked. Despite their recent challenges, Jim still loved Maggie.

"Don't, Jim," Maggie said.

"Don't what?"

"Just don't. Don't disappoint them again."

"Again?" Jim raised his voice.

"Thanksgiving, Matt's Little League championship and—"

"You know there was an emergency meeting that came up the night before the Little League thing," Jim said.

Maggie shook her head and exhaled. "I don't want to get into another argument over this. Just get here at ten. Bye."

Click.

Maggie was gone. Jim hung up and sat motionless. Maybe he should leave now. If he hurried, he could arrive by four, but Montgomery Plaza jumped back into his thoughts. He went out on a limb to get that project. He had to deliver, and if he succeeded, it was the type of deal that could boost his career even further.

Jim picked the phone back up and dialed. As the phone rang, he scanned several presents from corporate clients on the credenza. A fruitcake caught his eye. He sneered, picked up the speckled mess, and tossed it into the nearby wastebasket. *Who gives fruitcake as a gift anymore?*

"Guess who?" Jim said and listened for a response.

"Yeah, I love you too," he quipped with zero emotion. Jim glanced at another present, a fine bottle of Macallan scotch. "I gotta see you earlier than we planned." He inspected the label on the bottle and nodded. Now there was a gift. "The sooner, the better." Jim picked up another present, a box of cigars. "How about the Grotto, 1:00?" He sniffed the stogies and reacted—stale and disgusting. "Meet me out back."

Jim hung up and smelled the cigars again. Yep, still bad.

THE GROTTO WAS A HIGH-END STEAKHOUSE. Behind the restaurant, wooden crates, cardboard boxes, and plastic bags of refuse surrounded Jim in his black Armani suit as he puffed away on a Camel straight. The box of cigars rested on a crate beside him.

Charlie, equally well dressed, sauntered through the back door. "Alright, Jimbo, what's so damn important you gotta drag my ass into some filthy back alley?"

"Is that any way to greet an old friend?" Jim asked, and offered Charlie a cigarette.

"Old friend, huh?" Charlie slipped one out of the pack. Jim whipped out a zippo, and Charlie leaned forward and lit it. "Why do I only hear from my 'old friend' when he needs something?" He took a heavy drag and blew a giant billow of smoke.

Jim touched his heart as if the comment was a dagger. "Ouch. I thought it would be nice to catch up before the holidays... and I wanted to give you your present." He patted the box of cigars before handing it over.

Charlie studied the gift for a moment and smirked. Definitely up to his standards. "Thanks."

Jim smiled, knowing he'd impressed Charlie and made him feel guilty at the same time. "How's business been treating you?"

Charlie side-eyed Jim, his guard back up. "Business is great. How's yours?"

"It's great," Jim said. "It'd be a lot better if I land Montgomery Plaza."

"Is that right?" Charlie took another drag with the cigarette hanging off his lip.

"Hey, isn't your company bidding on Montgomery Plaza? Who's working that deal for you guys?"

Charlie shot Jim a look.

"You? Quite a coincidence. Nice piece of property, don't you think?"

"More like a piece of crap," Charlie said.

Jim shook his head as if pondering, but his thoughts and plan were crystal clear. "Yeah, I guess you're right. Seems like a waste, huh? Both companies bidding the price up so neither will make a profit."

"Not my dime." Charlie eyed the door, hoping they could go back inside and enjoy some nice filets.

The clock on this negotiation was running out. Jim had to find a way to close the deal. "It could be."

"What are you talking about?" Charlie asked.

"A little supplemental income for a small favor?"

"No such thing as a small favor with you, Jimbo."

Jim hated that nickname. He'd always felt it was Charlie's way of belittling him, even though he made twice as much money as Charlie. And Jim had won in other ways, but now was not the time for petty squabbles. "So, maybe we should make it a more substantial contribution for your efforts. How about $100,000?"

Charlie froze. Jim had his attention. "And how do you plan on coming up with a hundred grand?"

"Don't worry about it."

"Thanks, but no thanks," Charlie said.

"All you gotta do is make sure Vanstar doesn't bid higher than fifty million."

"Oh, is that all? Put my career on the line. And how do I accomplish this small feat?"

"Simple. Change a few numbers here and there." Jim waved his hand back and forth as if that was all it took. "They're only estimates."

Charlie shook his head. He wasn't biting. "Estimates based on a boatload of research."

Jim leaned in, trying to connect with Charlie. "It's not a big deal. Instead of assuming rents will increase at 5%, say 3%. Focus on the deteriorating area. You can justify it."

"Forget it, Jim."

Jim took another draft of his cigarette. "Don't decide this second. Think about it, okay?" He leaned back against a crate with his feet crossed, as if waiting for Charlie to come to his senses.

"You're unbelievable."

Jim continued to wait.

"I'm not doing it," Charlie said.

Jim's soft-sell wasn't working. Without Charlie on board, he had little chance of pulling off the deal. Jim panicked, but couldn't let it show. Never let 'em see you sweat was a cliché for a reason. He needed to project complete and total confidence while shifting to a new tactic. "Fine. I thought I was doing you a favor. I heard you were strapped for cash."

"Is that what you heard?"

Jim shrugged, knowing the dig had its desired effect. The two took drafts from their cigs.

"So, how's Maggie?"

"She left me." Jim looked down at the filthy ground. The reminder of his separation irritated Jim, but it also triggered an idea.

"Sorry," Charlie said, and he meant it.

"It happens. Who knows, maybe you'll get another crack at her." Jim chuckled.

Charlie yanked the cigarette out of his mouth and pointed it at Jim. He was about to hurl an insult back, but paused. "Why don't you make it $150,000?"

Jim rubbed his forehead in feigned shock. "$150,000! Geez, Chuck, I thought we were friends."

Charlie wasn't going to budge in his counter offer, especially after the Maggie potshot, but Jim didn't care. He had Charlie thinking with his emotions, and that's when people lose.

"$150,000 is fair, I guess. I can make it happen. But you're buying lunch." Jim took one more puff of his cigarette before dropping it and stomping it out. He'd gotten what he came for. A fifty dollar filet mignon was just a bonus.

CHAPTER THREE

JIM REVVED THE ENGINE OF HIS PORSCHE CARRERA and weaved in and out of traffic on his way back from lunch. The car was one of Jim's many perks—added bonuses for a job well done. He could only imagine the luxuries that awaited if he closed the Montgomery deal. With step one completed, his mind shifted into over-drive, coming up with ways to find the $150,000. One important business lesson he learned early in his career was that money was relative. In isolation, $150,000 was a big number, but it became small when compared to an enormous one. Few people truly grasp this concept because they only view the world from their limited perspective. In a deal worth a few thousand bucks, or even a million, $150,000 is a lot of money, but in a transaction where tens of millions of dollars are at stake, $150,000 is a rounding error. It's why the rich get richer. With seven-figure salaries, the wealthy can receive a meager two percent raise, and the increase totals more than many peoples' entire annual income.

Jim approached the gated parking structure of the Banner building and slid his ID card through the scanner. The gate opened, and he guided his car downward into the high-end garage.

As Jim cruised down to the larger reserved spaces, he passed the cars of executives from other companies. The first automobile was a Buick LeSabre. "Middle management," Jim mocked. Up next was a Lexus LS 400. "Toyota in a rented tux, no thanks." A Pontiac Bonneville followed. "Maybe when I'm eighty... and senile." A fourth car came into view, one he'd not seen before—a beat-up 1990 Chevrolet Camaro. "And what do we have here? Talk about a hillbilly hotrod." The nameplate on the parking spot read, *"Security."*

Jim parked nearby in his reserved space. After riding up the elevator to the ground floor, he passed Keith Campanero, a fifty-year-old security guard. A big teddy bear of a man, Keith looked like he'd have a hard time guarding against a cold.

"Good morning, sir," Keith greeted.

"Morning. You the new guard?" Jim asked as he pressed the up button on the main elevator.

"Yes, sir. Keith Campanero's the name. Started on Monday."

"Oh. So, that classic Camaro I just saw is yours, right?" Jim asked.

"That's my girl. I love that car, although I've had my eye on one of the newer models for some time now."

"Well, don't go mortgaging the house," Jim said.

"I won't. With a little hard work during the holidays, I should be able to manage."

The elevator arrived, and the doors opened. Jim

stepped in and chuckled. "McDonald's value menu for you and the Mrs. for the next few years, huh?"

Keith offered a polite smile.

"See you around, Keith." Jim pressed the button for the fiftieth floor.

After the sixty-second ride to the top floor, Jim sauntered through the bullpen on his way to the company kitchen. He passed a locked door marked "File Room" and eyed it. That room contained the key to accomplishing the next step in his plan to land Montgomery Plaza.

Out of nowhere, a twenty-something intern in a polo shirt and khakis turned the corner and smacked into Jim's chest. "I'm sorry, Mr. Sloane. I was in a rush to get this into the FedEx bin before the two o'clock pick up." The intern held up a pile of envelopes as proof.

Jim sneered at the intern, straightened his suit, and then continued on his way.

"Um, Mr. Sloane," the intern called out.

Jim stopped, exhaled deliberately loud, and turned.

"I was wondering if I to talk with you sometime for like five minutes about how you got started—any advice you might have?"

"What's your name?" Jim asked.

"William."

"How long have you been interning?"

"I started fall semester."

"Oh yeah!" Jim said with feigned interest. "You want my advice? Make a better first impression." He pointed to the mail room. "It's 2:04."

William scurried off as Jim moved on and entered

the kitchen. He set his briefcase down and poured himself a steaming cup of coffee—time to get rejuvenated with caffeine after his steak lunch.

Sam walked in, creating instant tension.

"Sammy boy, how's it going? Any plans for the holidays?" Jim asked, hoping to lighten the mood.

"Just staying home with the family."

Jim grinned and rolled his eyes. He knew that drill. Slow time at home can make a few days seem like a few months.

"I'm heading out soon," Sam said.

"Sounds good." Jim tapped the cup of his coffee and debated whether he should bring up the morning meeting. "Sam, buddy, I hope there are no hard feelings over the Montgomery deal."

Sam took a deep breath. "Not at all."

"You really did an amazing job crunching the numbers."

"Thanks."

"I mean it. Once you get a little more fire—get a little hungrier to make the deals work—you'll break out of that middle management rut."

Sam filled a cup of water and offered a forced smile on his way out. "Merry Christmas, Jim."

Now alone, Jim shrugged his shoulders and held up his hands, unsure why Sam failed to appreciate his advice.

Jim exited and passed through the bullpen towards Robert's office. Inside, various plaques, awards, and newspaper clippings adorned the walls. Included among them were a Purple Heart, a Bronze Star, and a Prisoner of War Medal that Robert earned as a Marine during the Vietnam War. It was like a museum that archived Robert's life, but the decorations weren't displayed to show-off or brag. They reminded Robert of his humble beginnings and the challenges he'd overcome. Overall, the office was modest compared to Jim's lavish tastes. It could have been the work space of a small business owner, even though Robert's net worth exceeded a hundred million dollars.

Robert packed his briefcase when Jim knocked on the open door. "Jim, come in. What's on your mind?"

"Just wanted to thank you for the opportunity on the Montgomery deal."

Robert smiled. "You earned it."

"Thanks."

Robert gathered his things to leave. "Well, I'm off to meet the wife. We're heading down to Cabo for the holidays. If you want to beat the holiday traffic, I'd suggest you head out too."

"I'll be out of here in a bit. I want to get a jump start on the paperwork."

"Montgomery Plaza will be here when you get back," Robert said.

"I know. I won't stay too late."

Robert put his briefcase down and grabbed Jim by the shoulders. "Jim, listen to me. Go. Forget about work. Spend some time with your family. Your efforts on the company's behalf don't go unnoticed."

Jim motioned to Robert's briefcase. "I see I'm not the only one doing a little work over the holidays?"

"Guilty as charged. Just a few forms to take care of for the SEC reviewer next week, then it's all fun in the sun. You should do the same."

Jim looked down and nodded, as if he was considering Robert's advice, which he wasn't. "Maybe you're right. Thanks, Robert. You need a hand with anything?"

"No, I've got it. Take care and have a merry Christmas." Robert left.

"You, too."

Robert deliberately took the long way through the bullpen and wished the secretaries and staff happy holidays. When he was out of sight, Jim marched back to his office and passed Sharon. Time to get things done. "Sharon, did you get Sam's files?"

"On your desk," she said.

Jim entered his office and found a Hispanic janitor emptying his garbage can while jamming to an old handheld radio sticking out of his rear pocket.

"Hey, amigo," Jim said.

The janitor didn't hear him. Jim tapped him on the shoulder.

"Hey, amigo!"

Startled, the janitor clicked the radio off. "Name Eduardo." He spoke in broken-English with a heavy Spanish accent.

"Aren't you a little early?" Jim asked.

"We told half day. Start cleaning—2:00. Holiday."

Jim patted Eduardo on the back. "Okay, I only understood about half that, but not this office now, okay, amigo." Jim enunciated in a slow and louder than normal voice. "Come back at your usual hour. Normal time, comprende?"

Eduardo nodded and exited.

Jim called out, "I expect this office to be clean when I get back next week."

Jim sat down and dove into the Montgomery Plaza files. He didn't get too far before Sharon entered and interrupted.

"Jim, have a good holiday. I'll see you next Monday," she said, with her purse and keys in hand.

Jim glanced up and furrowed his brow. "Where are you going?"

"Remember I told you last week I was picking my sister up in Pittsburgh, and then we were driving down to Harrisburg to surprise our mom for Christmas? My car was having trouble starting this morning, so I need to get it into the shop."

"But we're a team, and we just got assigned Mont-gomery Plaza. You're like my right hand. I need you."

Sharon blushed and warmed to Jim's words.

"I might need some copying or faxing or someone to place calls," Jim said.

Sharon pursed her lips. Any sense that Jim was complimenting her vanished.

"A bit longer, okay?" Jim asked, even though it wasn't a question.

Deflated, Sharon trudged back to her cubicle.

Over the next several hours, staff members gathered their things. One-by-one they left to go home. By 6:30, only Jim and Sharon remained. Jim toiled away in his office while Sharon sputtered on the phone. "I know it's too late now. He ruined everything." She glanced towards Jim's ostentatious oak doors with daggers in her eyes. "He knows. I told him. I don't need a new job. I need a new boss." She chuckled. "I wish. Okay. I'll tell him." Sharon hung up, took a deep breath to muster her courage, and entered Jim's office. "Jim, I have to go. I'm three hours late."

Engrossed with work, Jim didn't even look up. "Okay, fine."

"Have a wonderful holiday," Sharon said without meaning it.

"Uh-huh," Jim responded, not listening or caring.

Sharon exited in a huff. When the main doors slammed shut, Jim's eyes darted up from the file. Time to finish what he needed to get done. He rose to his feet, left his office, and scanned the bullpen. Jim was alone.

He passed through the cubicles and made a beeline to the door marked "File Room." He pulled out his keys and unlocked the door, revealing rows and rows of file cabinets that reached the ceiling. Jim perused the labels on the cabinets until he spotted the one marked "Company Financials." He opened the drawer and removed several "First Quarter Budget" files with "Confidential" stamped on the front. Jim began reading one on his way back to his office. Engrossed in the classified details, he plopped down at his desk and scanned page after page. Jim compared figures, scoured expense reports, and mined the data. He punched some numbers into an Excel spreadsheet, and the number 151,353 popped up.

"Bingo." Jim stretched with a gleam of satisfaction in his eye until his gaze fell on the clock—7:45. He groaned before picking up the phone and dialing.

Maggie sat in a recliner reading a romance novel as her two boys battled it out on their Playstation. Her cell phone rang. She clicked the button and answered, "Hello."

"Hey, Maggie," Jim said in as cheerful a voice as possible.

"Jim? Are you at the airport?"

"No, I got tied up at work. I'm going to take a morning flight."

Maggie stood and walked into the kitchen, out of earshot of the kids. "You better be kidding, Jim."

"I'm sorry. Look, I'll get there first thing tomorrow. It'll be okay."

Maggie shook her head. The last straw had been reached. "No, it won't be," she said, almost in a whisper.

"Sure, it will. You said it yourself. I wouldn't have seen them tonight, anyway."

"Not that, Jim." A tear streamed down Maggie's cheek. "This isn't working."

"What isn't?" Jim asked, knowing full well what she meant.

"Us. I'm tired of this. It's over."

"Maggie, stop it. I don't need this right now. I've got a lot going on at work."

"I can't do this anymore."

Jim gritted his teeth and gripped the phone so tight he almost crushed it. "This is unbelievable. Just because I've been busting my ass so you can shop five days a week—"

"Come on, Jim."

Jim continued to hurl insults. "Have lattes with the girls."

"Stop."

"Your own personal trainer. Does he give you private lessons, Maggie?"

"What's that supposed to mean?" Maggie asked.

"What do you think?"

Maggie snapped back, "At least he'd be around to get the job done."

Silenced into submission, Jim collected himself and tried a softer approach. "I'm sorry, Maggie. I didn't mean it. Let's talk about this when I get there. It's been a long day. You're tired. I'm exhausted. Things will be better tomorrow."

Maggie's head drooped, and she covered her face with her hand, even though no one was around to see her tears. "Jim, we're lying to ourselves. You're not going to change. I'm tired of being second—I've been tired. We'll put on a happy face through Christmas for the kids, but after that... I want to make it official. I want a divorce."

CHAPTER FOUR

FOUR SMALL WORDS—I WANT A DIVORCE—CAUSED Jim's confident business bravado to vanish in an instant. Sure, he still wore a three thousand dollar suit, and his office decor totaled more than most people's income, but right now, at this moment, he was nothing more than a soon-to-be divorced middle-aged man, sitting alone in his office at Christmas time. Jim held the phone and tried to come up with one good reason why Maggie should change her mind, but he couldn't muster a peep. He hung up, defeated.

Jim dragged himself into his private restroom. He turned on the faucet and splashed cool water on his face until he caught his reflection in the mirror. Who was that dejected guy staring back? And what did he do to deserve this? Jim tortured himself by imagining Maggie and the boys having Christmas without him. They had a Christmas tradition, where they'd take a family photo which would become a mantle decoration for future Christmases. Over the years, the custom created a time-lapse of sorts. The mantle pictures started with Jim and Maggie's first Christmas together and continued through last year's holiday with their two boys. If Jim was lucky, he might be in one more photo.

He left the bathroom and gathered the confidential files off his desk. After a long day, it was time to head out and start the holidays. Maggie might not be happy to see him, but his boys would be, and that would have to do—at least for now. Jim pulled on the handcrafted brass handle on one of the doors, but it didn't budge. The door was locked. He tugged again, but it wasn't moving. He reached into his pocket and searched for his keys before remembering he'd left them in the file room door. But that didn't explain who locked his office.

Jim banged on the door. "Sharon, are you still here?"

Silence.

Jim banged louder.

Still silence.

Jim racked his brain, trying to remember the name of the janitor. "Hey, amigo! You locked me in." The name dawned on Jim. "Hey, Eduardo! Pal!"

Jim smashed his fist against the door. "Open the damn door!" He rushed back to his desk and picked up the phone. It was dead. "What the hell?"

He searched through his briefcase for his iPhone. It wasn't in the usual pocket where he kept it. He dumped the entire briefcase over, spilling all the contents onto the floor. There was no iPhone among the mess.

Jim slammed the empty briefcase shut and tossed it aside. He slumped down in his seat and peered at his computer screen when he realized—another way out.

Jim pulled up his email and clicked on the "New Message" icon.

He typed Maggie's address and added the following message: *Maggie. I'm locked in my office. The phones are down. Please call someone for me. Jim.*

Jim didn't bother proofreading and pressed the "Send" button. A moment later, a return email popped into his inbox with the subject line: *Undeliverable Message. Server Not Responding.*

Jim threw up his hands with a disgusted smile. He should have guessed as much. Jim surveyed the office for other ideas, and the fax machine caught his eye. The antique device might be his ticket out of here.

Jim grabbed a sheet of paper and a pen. "Security has still gotta be here. What the hell is the name of that tubby guard?" He tapped the paper with the pen until it came to him. "Keith!" Jim scrawled a message: *Keith. Locked in. Come open my office door immediately!!! 50th Floor Suite 5003. Jim Sloane.*

He checked the building's phone sheet posted behind him and found security's fax number. He then stared at the machine, confused. "I told you I might need you, Sharon." Jim pressed the numbers for security, then laid the paper on the tray. Nothing happened. "Go!" His shouting did nothing, of course, which only infuriated Jim further. He inspected the machine again, then pressed the green "Start" button. The machine came to life and sucked the document into its bowels before spitting it back out.

Jim offered a relieved smile. He fell back into his leather chair and waited. A few moments later, the machine ejected a fax confirmation. Jim snatched it. *Error, No Dial Tone. Transmission Incomplete.*

Jim crumpled the paper and flung it into the wastebasket. He searched the office for more ideas. Security had to be around somewhere. They must be making rounds. At least, that's what he hoped. Jim seized a sheet of paper from the printer and scribbled: *HELP! I'm locked in. Please open my door.*

He slid the paper under the oak doors and then stood for a moment, expecting someone to see the note immediately. No one came.

With nothing left to do, his anger boiled over. "Open the doors now!" Jim shoved the doors. Not much movement, but enough to encourage him to try to bowl his way through. He lowered his shoulder and rammed into the heavy wood. After several attempts, the only thing he accomplished was making his shoulder sore. He paused and collected his thoughts. He was going to have to think his way out. Jim surveyed the room again for anything useful.

An idea.

He hurried over to his desk and rummaged through drawers. He found old company pamphlets, a letter opener, an old pack of cigarettes, and an empty macaroni picture frame that read, *"Happy Father's Day."* The sentimental keepsake paused Jim for a moment, but then he tossed it aside. Not much use for what he had in mind. He disappeared into the bathroom, and after a loud crash, he returned with the metal rod from the towel rack. Jim slid the rod through the door handles and used it for leverage to rip the brass handles off. He put all his strength into the effort, but the thin rod buckled and bent. Jim flung the twisted metal aside and rubbed his forehead. He was stuck, locked in for the night.

After accepting the situation, Jim surveyed his posh office. It could be worse. He picked up a cup from his small executive bar and opened the Macallan scotch. After pouring himself a tall glass, he sat down on his black leather couch, loosened his tie, kicked off his shoes, and took a healthy sip. "Somebody's ass is getting fired tomorrow, and it ain't me, amigo."

The minutes passed and Jim continued sipping the high-end liquor alone and in silence. It had been a long day, both from work and the emotional toll of his marriage ending. His eyelids grew heavy, and he gave in to sleep.

MORNING CAME and Jim awoke on the sofa with the bottle of scotch, now a quarter empty, next to him. With tired eyes, he pulled himself to his feet and tested the doors. Still locked. He dropped to his knees, leaned his head against the carpet, and peered through the slit under the door. His piece of paper was still there. He shook his head. Ridiculous.

Jim dragged himself into the bathroom, unzipped and relieved himself. When he finished, he pulled the lever to flush the toilet. *Bawoosh*. The water swirled and disappeared down the drain, but it didn't reset. The bowl remained empty. Jim jiggled the handle, hoping for a quick fix to the problem, but nothing happened. He smacked the top of the toilet and gave up. It was already one of those days.

Jim turned the faucet on to wash his hands, but nothing came out. He chuckled to himself. Unbelievable.

He left the restroom and checked the time—8:15. Jim banged his fist against the wall. "I can't wait to tell this one to Maggie. Hey hon, I missed my flight because some nit wit locked me in my office."

He rechecked the phone. Still dead. "You gotta be kidding. Where the hell is security?" Jim's gaze fell on the little Christmas tree in the corner of his office. He looked at his day planner and remembered—it was the holiday weekend. Jim inspected the dates closer with his finger. It was Saturday, December 23rd, and the office was closed until Wednesday, the 27th. Security wasn't making rounds.

A worried look crept across Jim's face as he fell back in his chair. This was no longer just an inconvenience. He might be trapped in his office for another four days. Jim tilted his head up to the heavens for some divine intervention and noticed the smoke detector on the ceiling. He jumped to his feet, pulled one of the guest chairs underneath, and climbed up. Jim held his lighter next to the sensor and covered his head with his jacket for the impending downpour.

Nothing.

He pulled out a cigarette from his pocket, lit up, then took a heavy drag and blew the smoke on the sensor.

The phone rang and startled Jim. "It's about time."

He hopped down and picked up the receiver. "This is Jim."

An electronically garbled voice said, "The fire alarm and sprinkler system are turned off. If you start a fire, you'll burn or asphyxiate before help arrives."

"Who is this?" Jim demanded.

"The Ghost of Christmas Past," the voice taunted.

"What kind of sick joke—"

"This is no joke, Jim. Without food or water, the cleaning crew will only find a corpse come Wednesday morning.

Click.

The phone went dead.

CHAPTER FIVE

FOR THE FIRST TIME, FEAR SETTLED INTO JIM'S stomach, which left him queasy and his legs shaky. Someone had done this on purpose. Did this person really want him dead? His fear turned to anger and a burning resolve—no one toyed with him. He stormed over to the door and kicked it several times. *Smack. Smack. Smack.* Each time, his foot thudded off the heavy wood. "Come on!"

But the door didn't give an inch. "This is ridiculous!"

Accepting failure only for an instant, he hurried back to his desk and pulled up Microsoft Word on his computer.

His fingers raced as he typed a letter in a large, bold font. *Help, trapped on the 50th floor of the Banner Building. No food or water. Phones are dead. Please call the police.*

Jim pushed the printer towards the ventilation window, a two-and-a-half foot by one and a half foot piece of slatted glass that opened at the base of the giant glass window.

He turned the latch and cracked the window open about five inches. A biting breeze whipped into the office.

Jim shoved the printer in the opening. He tilted the front down by stuffing a book under the backside so the papers would eject out. Next, Jim pulled up the printer icon on his computer and set the number of copies to one hundred. With a satisfied grin, he moved the cursor to the "Print" button. As his finger pressed down on the mouse, the lights shut off, and the screen turned black. Jim pounded on the mouse button, hoping to will it into action. An eerie calm set in as Jim realized the coincidence of the timing. He was being watched.

Jim gritted his death. This was unacceptable. No one would watch him like some sort of television show. Jim scoured the office, looking for a camera or bugging device. He checked the walls, behind pictures, the carpet, the couches, light fixtures, and the vents. "Where are you hiding?"

Nothing.

With all options exhausted, Jim's gaze fell upon the skyline and the twin tower across the way. Nothing suspicious stood out, but it might be possible to keep tabs on him from there. But even if someone could spy on him like that, it still didn't explain the power outage. Without a better explanation, Jim's paranoia forced him to take action. He removed a large painting from the wall and leaned it against the window, covering a third of it.

He slid his couch behind the hidden part and sat down, hopefully alone and unwatched. After allowing himself to relax, Jim slumped back into the cushions.

His delusions and frustration gave way to exhaustion. It had been over fifteen hours since he consumed anything besides alcohol, and the effects were already noticeable. His mouth was dry, his energy low, and his mind foggy. A born fighter, Jim shrugged it off.

He marched to the printer, opened the tray, grabbed the paper, and returned to the couch. He then began the tedious process of writing his distress message by hand, one page at a time.

———

HEAVY CLOUDS ROLLED IN, and the morning drifted into the afternoon. With the power off, that meant no lights and no heat. Jim shivered from the cold and finished the last handwritten letter. Satisfied with the stack, he walked to the window and pulled the printer back.

"Shut this off, asshole." Jim tapped the glass with his middle finger for any prying eyes before tossing the papers out into the evening air. The pile descended and dissipated with individual letters flittering in every direction and settling throughout the park far below.

Pleased with his efforts, Jim wondered how long before someone found the notes. He pressed his forehead against the giant window pane and tried to look down, but the angle only allowed a quarter of the park to be visible. That wasn't enough for Jim. He inspected the small hinges on the bottom of the ventilation window. The entire unit could be pulled out if he could loosen or break the hinges.

Jim opted for choice number two. He grabbed a blue

agate paperweight off the desk and pounded the joints. After a few moments, the hinges twisted, and the joint screws popped out. The window dislodged and fell outward. The momentum carried it over the twelve-inch iron ledge that ran along the perimeter of each floor.

Jim reached through the opening, but he was too late. He slid himself outside and leaned over the ledge just in time to see the window fall the last few stories to the ground. The seven hundred foot drop gave Jim vertigo and a fear induced nausea. The view spiraled, and the cold added to the effect as an icy wind caused his eyes to water. He blinked several times, and his vision stopped spinning, but the nausea remained.

Far below, a figure emerged. Jim squinted and couldn't believe his luck. "Yes! Yes! Yes! Come on, buddy, get me out of here."

As he strained his eyes, the person moved systematically throughout the park and paused every so often. To Jim's horror, the figure didn't appear to be reacting. This person collected the letters. "What the hell are you doing?" Jim cupped his hands around his mouth and shouted down, "Hey, asshole!" But he was far too high for anyone to hear or see clearly.

Jim pulled himself inside, grabbed his scotch glass, slid back out, and hurled it down. The cup sailed down to the ground, and even though Jim couldn't hear it smash, his effort had the desired effect. The person scurried away.

The phone rang, and Jim answered.

"That wasn't very nice, Jim," the garbled voice said.

"For someone so fond of neatness, you should know that littering is illegal."

"Have fun picking glass out of your ass, pal."

"Insults aren't going to get you out of there. Of course, you're not going anywhere, anyway. And what makes you think it was me? Could have been the gardener or janitor just doing his job."

"What do you want? Why are you doing this to me?" Jim asked.

"Oh, why do bad things happen to good people? You couldn't possibly deserve this," the voice said.

"What are you talking about? I haven't done anything to you."

"Better hurry. Your time is running out, Jim."

Click.

CHAPTER SIX

Jim held the dead phone and pondered the identity of his captor. Coming up blank, a thought popped into his head, albeit a dangerous one. "No risk, no reward" was a business axiom that Jim lived by, and right now, he needed to focus on the reward—freedom. If he imagined the outcome of failure, he might not have the nerve for what he envisioned.

Jim went back to the window and peeked out. The twelve-inch iron ledge ran the perimeter of the floor. About twenty-five feet to the left, a thin concrete pillar jutted out, marking the end of his office and the start of another.

Jim pulled himself inside and slipped the agate paperweight into his pocket. He attempted to slide his entire body out the window and onto the ledge, but he discovered that sticking his head out was far easier than getting his whole body out. He angled himself sideways, careful not to extend too much of his torso over the ledge.

Once outside, the cold blasted him. Jim climbed to his feet, and he shivered from both the temperature and dread. Already having second thoughts, Jim coaxed himself along. "Come on. Nice and easy."

He leaned his weight back against the glass and sidled down the ledge with baby steps. Every few seconds, a gust of wind tested his balance. Jim remained focused and kept his eyes straight ahead, never down. Step-by-step, he moved towards his goal. Soon, his hand rubbed against the pillar that signaled the end of his office. He grabbed hold and collected himself.

Jim turned his head and assessed the pillar, determining how best to navigate the obstacle. He then swiveled his body around it with his right foot leading the way.

As he shifted his weight, he glimpsed the fall that awaited should he err. A shot of adrenaline spiked through his veins. Petrified and breathing fast, he pulled himself back. This maneuver would require most of his body to extend beyond the ledge, and there would be a moment when all of his weight would be on one leg. If a big gust of wind hit and he lost his balance, it would be game over.

No risk, no reward. Those words kept playing in Jim's head. He needed to do this. If successful, he could be free in minutes. Jim calmed himself down and made a second attempt, this time keeping his eyes glued to the concrete pillar. He swung his right foot around and felt for the other side. Once he planted it, he shifted his weight, then brought his left around and completed the maneuver. He breathed an enormous sigh of relief.

Now facing the glass, Jim looked inside. It was

Robert's office. It seemed so inviting with its plaques, awards, and, most importantly, the open door.

Jim removed the paperweight from his pants and gripped it in his palm. He cocked his arm and smacked the side of the window. Without leverage, the blow had little force behind it and resulted in a muted thud. Jim reared his arm further and struck the glass with more oomph.

Still nothing.

Now worried and frustrated, Jim separated his feet wider for added leverage. The heel of his right foot hung just over the ledge. He pulled the paperweight back and whipped it forward against the glass. The blow slammed against the window, but the thick glass deflected his arm, causing his weight to shift precariously. His left foot stepped back to steady himself. Both feet now danced dangerously on the edge. As he flailed for balance, he dropped the paperweight, and his hand grazed the concrete pillar. His fingers locked onto it.

Jim huddled down in the corner next to the pillar, breathing hard and shaking. The terror overwhelmed him and his body heaved and vomited, but having not eaten anything in over a day, only bits of food and stomach acid leaked onto the ledge.

Jim wiped his mouth and collected his thoughts. Now what? Once sane enough to think, Jim discovered he was squatting in front of Robert's ventilation window. He wondered if, like his own, he could push it open. Jim tapped on the small window with his fist, careful not to make the same mistake twice. "Come on," he pleaded. He banged a little harder. Nothing doing.

The window was latched shut from the inside. Jim pounded along the frame of the window. But it, too, was unyielding. Deep down, Jim knew the idea would fail, but he didn't want to admit to himself that his only option was to return to his office.

He summoned his courage and strength, grabbed the pillar, and got to his feet. With shaky legs, he took a breath and extended his left foot around until his toe connected with the other side of the ledge. The wind kicked up and taunted him. Jim prayed for it to remain calm and continued the maneuver. Once he planted his left foot, he shifted his weight and slid back around. He then sidled across the ledge, squatted down, and wriggled his way into his office.

Jim collapsed onto his couch. His lavish and once comfortable office had now become his personal prison.

The phone rang.

Jim picked up the guest phone on the side table, knowing full well his tormentor was on the other end.

"You could get yourself killed trying something like that," the mysterious voice mocked.

"Or maybe get myself out," Jim said.

"Were you trying to fly your way out with that crazy arm flailing? I know you're not dumb enough to try to break two-inch-thick commercial grade glass. Or maybe you are."

"Is there any point to all this?" Jim asked. "Why don't you save us both a lot of time and energy? What do you say? What's this all about?"

"Sorry, Jim, your wheeling and dealing isn't going to work here."

"Who's wheeling? I'd just like to know who I'm speaking with."

"This isn't about me. This is about what you've done. If you want to find a way out in time, you'd better think about that."

Click.

CHAPTER SEVEN

THE SUN SLIPPED BELOW THE HORIZON. NIGHT WAS coming, and it was bringing a freezing cold.

Already feeling the effects of dehydration, Jim disappeared into the bathroom to hunt for any water he might have missed. He removed the tank cover from the toilet and peered inside. Empty. Jim ran his fingers along the bottom and gathered a few droplets of residual moisture. He grimaced at the toilet water, but sucked it down. Frustrated, he ambled out of the bathroom and fell onto the couch.

Jim picked up the letter opener and tried to wedge it under the paneling on the wall. Perhaps he could tunnel his way out. His efforts yielded no immediate results because of the hard Brazilian cherry wood and expert craftsmanship. Next, he tried chipping away at it. After several strikes, he inspected the wall—barely a mark. "This will take all day." He chuckled, realizing he might have three. He swung his legs on the couch, got himself comfortable, and began scraping away.

The last hint of sunlight faded, and the office darkened. If not for the faint glow from the city lights, it would be pitch black. The freezing cold didn't help matters, either.

Jim's scraping and chipping yielded modest results. He paused for a moment, squinted his eyes, and rubbed his fingers across the small scar. "Why did I get the damn cherry wood?"

Exhausted, he tossed the letter opener aside.

With the power off, Jim sat in darkness, shivering as the temperature continued to drop. Biting wind swirled into the office through the open ventilation window, wearing him down like Chinese water torture.

Outside, gusts of snow raced by the main window. Arms held close together to keep warm, he lumbered over to the opening, leaned out on the ledge, and opened his mouth. Only a few flakes settled on his tongue.

Jim slid back inside, grabbed a plastic filing tray, and placed it on the ledge to catch the snow. He perched himself by the window to survey the results. A handful of flakes fell on the tray before a blast of wind blew it away.

Jim pounded his fist against the glass and then scoured the office for a replacement. He seized his cup-shaped crystal pen holder and tested its weight. Satisfied it wouldn't blow away, he placed it on the ledge. The shape of the cup and strong wind made for a less than ideal collection container as most of the snow flew past. A flake or two found the target, but anything meaningful would take hours.

Jim shifted his focus to keeping warm. He pushed the printer against the open space, which blocked about half of it, but not enough to make much of a difference. Jim opened a drawer and grabbed a couple of books —*The Seven Habits of Highly Effective People* and *Negotiate Your Way To The Top*. Jim wedged them between the side of the printer and window, then stood back to survey the results.

The two small books did little to block the remaining opening, but with less space, the wind now whistled in with each gust.

Jim scanned the office again and grabbed one of the smaller couch cushions. He crammed it into the space on the other side of the printer. The wind still whistled around the edges, but it was an improvement.

The temperature continued to drop. Jim blew on his hands to keep them warm, but things were going to get a lot colder before the night was through. He needed a heat source.

IN THE DEAD OF NIGHT, the eastern tower was almost entirely dark. One bit of light, an orangish glow, emanated from an office on the top floor—Jim's office.

Huddled in the middle of the room, Jim sat on one of the couch cushions in front of a crackling fire he'd built in the metal trash can. He fed the small inferno with the wooden drawers from his desk. Despite being in a lavish work space, light from the flames danced across Jim's face like a primal caveman. He stared at the embers and mulled over suspects. Who could be responsible for this sadistic crime? Eduardo, the janitor, came to mind as Jim replayed the taunting voice in his head. *And what makes you think it was me out there? Could have been the park's gardener or janitor just doing their job.*

Jim imagined Eduardo sneaking up to his door, locking it with a vindicated grin, and then sitting in the janitor's closet drinking a Corona with a dirty rag over the phone. In his thick, difficult-to-understand Spanish accent, Eduardo taunted, "This no joke, Jim. With no food and no water, cleaning crew only find corpse on Wednesday."

Jim shook his head and laughed at his delusion. But maybe it was possible. Jim tossed another desk drawer in the wastebasket, causing the smoke in the office to thicken. He didn't notice as his mind continued to wander and consider possibilities.

Jim pictured a deranged Sharon, on the phone with a napkin over the speaker, gorging on a gigantic brownie, her desk a complete sty. She altered her voice to sound deep and coarse. "That wasn't very nice, Jim. For someone so fond of neatness, you should know that littering is illegal."

"Have fun picking glass out of your ass, pal," Jim said.

Sharon grimaced. "Insults aren't going to get you out of there. Of course, you're not going anywhere, anyway." She took a big, defiant bite out of her brownie.

Jim laughed at the ridiculousness of the thought. He coughed and choked from the layer of smoke above him, then shrugged it off as the mysterious voice played back in his head. *Oh, why do bad things happen to good people? You couldn't possibly deserve this.*

The voice had also said something else, something odd and cryptic. When Jim asked who he was speaking with, the voice responded, "The Ghost of Christmas Past."

CHAPTER EIGHT

TEN YEARS AGO, ALMOST TO THE DAY, A YOUNGER, more vibrant version of Jim sat in Robert Banner's office wearing a bargain basement suit in need of a good press. Robert leaned back in his chair and browsed Jim's resume. "You worked for Pennington."

"That's right," Jim said.

Robert continued perusing aloud, "Integrated new information management system." He smiled, reading between the lines. "Sounds impressive. What exactly does that mean?"

Blood rushed to Jim's face, embarrassed to admit the truth. "It was a different way to file."

"I see. Graduated from Long Beach City College."

Jim nodded as he bit his lip and tapped his finger against the armrest of the chair. The job was slipping away.

"Good school. Do you know what my alma mater was?"

"United States Marine Corps, sir," Jim answered. "You enlisted right after high school."

Robert raised an eyebrow. "A candidate who does his homework. I like that."

Jim cracked a smile, his confidence boosted. "Served two tours in Vietnam and spent four months in a POW camp before coming home and starting Banner Real Estate."

Robert grew quiet for a moment. Maybe Jim had pressed too much.

"The four longest months of my life," Robert said. "Made the business world look like child's play. Anyway, I'm sure you can appreciate that we can pick and choose our candidates from all the finest universities."

Jim clenched his jaw, having heard speeches like this before.

"Of course, that doesn't mean shit in my book," Robert said with a wry smile.

Jim's eyes lit up.

"The secret to success is getting out there and doing it. You learn what you're made of when your ass is on the line—under fire, so to speak. We get dozens of snot-nosed Ivy Leaguers who still have their silver spoon dangling from their mouth."

Jim nodded and leaned forward.

"They've all worked for top firms, which shows me nothing more than daddy can make a few phone calls. What I'm looking for is someone with fire and passion. Someone who has a good work ethic and doesn't want things handed to them," Robert said.

"That's why I applied, sir." Jim grinned. After months of scanning job websites, filling out applications, and interviewing, Jim was finally going to get a job offer.

"Unfortunately, we just filled our last spot a week ago."

Jim's face dropped. "I see."

"But I like you, Jim, and we're always looking for good people here. I'm going to hold on to your resume in case something opens up.

Jim stood and shook Robert's hand. "I'd appreciate that. Thank you for the interview."

"My pleasure," Robert said.

Jim left Robert's office and did his best to conceal his disappointment.

On his way out, Jim passed by the copy room and a voice called out, "Jim Sloane."

Jim turned and recognized the individual. "Mark Jackson. What are you doing here?" he asked in a forced, upbeat tone that hid his strong disdain for Mark.

"I work here. Just started a week ago. What about you?" Mark asked.

"I was here for an interview."

"I didn't think there were any positions left," Mark said.

"There aren't." Jim looked Mark in the eye. He knew Mark was mocking him.

"That's too bad. It would have been great to have you aboard," Mark said.

Jim shrugged. "Oh, well. Things will work out for the best."

"That's the spirit. Take care, Jimmy boy." Mark patted Jim on the shoulder and then sauntered down the hallway, but to Jim it seemed like was skipping, just to rub it in.

Jim bit his tongue, but his expression read like an open book. What a jerk!

THE SMOKE BROUGHT Jim back to reality as he coughed and sputtered. If he kept the fire going, he'd suffocate. He yanked the printer from the window and stuck his head out in the freezing but fresh night air. After a few breaths, he checked his water collection efforts, and discovered only a few drops in the cup holder.

He pulled himself inside, grateful to find the smoke had already thinned out. But as the fire died down, the temperature dropped, and it got a lot darker. Jim needed another heat and light source.

Jim grabbed the letter opener and bottle of scotch and hunkered down on the floor with his back against the couch.

He poked a hole in the bottle cap with the letter opener. Next, Jim unlaced his left shoe and soaked the lace in the scotch. He placed one end in the bottle and threaded the other through the cap hole. Jim screwed the cap on, pulled out his zippo, and lit his makeshift wick.

"Eat your heart out, MacGyver," he said as the lace glowed with a blue flame for about three seconds before going out. Jim lit it again with the same result. His shoulders slumped. Can't anything go right?

Jim shoved the bottle away and studied the leather couch cushions. People wore leather all the time. Why couldn't he? He unzipped the coverings and pulled them off the cushions. With both covers in hand, he disappeared into the bathroom and shut the door to escape the blasts of whistling wind. After settling into the corner, Jim blanketed himself with the leather. It was warmer, but it was also pitch black. With his eyes unable to focus on anything, his thoughts drifted to Maggie and simpler times.

A MUCH YOUNGER MAGGIE PLACED MODEST Christmas decorations around their small, one-bedroom apartment that desperately needed renovation. She positioned a family of wooden reindeer on the end table beside the couch. A painting of children building a snowman replaced the generic mountain vista on the picture wall. A four foot fake Christmas tree sat beside the fireplace, and a handful of homemade ornaments hung off its bent branches. Maggie's finishing touch was putting up the photos of past Christmases on the mantel. The first picture was taken at a restaurant from one of the couple's first dates right before Christmas. Almost a year later, Jim proposed, and the second photo showed the beaming pair, with Maggie holding up her engagement ring. Their wedding photo, taken the year after, was the third photo on the mantle. The final picture, captured last year in front of the same sad little tree, was their first Christmas as husband and wife. Despite the less than luxurious setting, Jim and Maggie smiled and looked very much in love.

Jim entered the apartment with a small bouquet of

lilies that had already started to brown. He wore his best forced smile as he tossed his coat on the couch, gave Maggie a kiss, and handed her the bouquet. "For you, my dear."

"Lilies. Thank you, honey." Maggie smelled their soft citrus aroma.

"I love you," Jim said.

"And I love you," she said, with a twinkle in her eye. It was little things like this that made her fall in love with Jim. She motioned to the pictures on the mantle. "So what do you think?"

"Looks great."

Maggie stood back and admired the photos. "We're going to take our favorite picture from each Christmas, and when we're eighty, we'll need a home with ten fireplaces."

The idea of ten fireplaces soured Jim's mood. He couldn't afford the one they had. He drifted into the kitchen, which was a generous term as it consisted of a small cubby with an icebox refrigerator. Inside, Jim found economy foods like microwavable dinners. He ignored the meals, pulled out a Budweiser, and sat on a second-hand plaid sofa.

Maggie watched as she filled a vase with water. "Hon, it's okay."

"What is?" Jim said, trying to keep up a cheerful facade.

Maggie crossed the tiny room and gave him a hug. "It's fine that you didn't get the job."

"I just don't want you to worry."

"I'm not worried. You'll find something."

Jim wished he shared his wife's confidence. He took

a sip of beer. "I don't know. There's not much demand for a twenty-four-year-old with a city college degree and two internships in the mailroom."

"I believe in you."

"I know, and that's why I want to give you a nice house with ten fireplaces, a car—all the things you deserve." He flicked his wrist toward the vase of drooping flowers. "They were practically giving the lilies away."

Maggie leaned down and gave Jim a tender kiss. "Lilies are my favorite. Besides, all I want is you."

Jim smiled. At least he had one thing going well in his life. "I thought I might have had a chance at Banner & Brown, but they filled their last spot a couple weeks ago," Jim said, and then choked on his next sip of beer. "Oh, and you'll never guess who they hired."

"Who?" Maggie stood behind Jim and rubbed his shoulders.

"Do you remember Mark Jackson?"

"No!"

Jim nodded.

"How did he get a job?" Maggie asked. "From what I remember, if he wasn't high, he was getting bailed out of jail by his girlfriend."

"That was a long time ago, I guess. He seemed like he's cleaned up his act, but still...," Jim searched for the right words to sum up his feelings. "The guy is such an ass, and *he's* got a job."

"I know. Sooner or later, a guy like that gets what he deserves."

Jim did his best to shrug it off and forget about it by

savoring another swig of cheap beer. "Did we get any mail?"

"Uh... yeah. It's over there." Maggie motioned to a small pile of envelopes on the table. "I don't think there was anything important."

Too late. Jim already hopped to his feet and was at the table, flipping through the stack. Included were several bills with "Past Due" stamped on the front in bright red letters.

"Not important?" Jim held up a bill.

"If we need money, I can always go back to waitressing."

Jim swiped the air with his hand. "No way. Not when you're so close to getting your degree. I'll figure something out."

THE NEXT DAY, Jim walked the stone pathways at the University of Pennsylvania to a conservative five-story red brick building with a sign that read, *"Biddle Law Library."*

A perky blonde in a ponytail and glasses waited in front of the entrance.

"Hey, Cindy," Jim said. "Thanks for doing this. I really appreciate it."

"No problem. What are you looking for, anyway?" Cindy led Jim inside to a cluster of computers.

Jim stammered for a response, "Background research."

"Well, if you need anything else, let me know." Cindy leaned over a computer and pulled up Lexis-

Nexis, a searchable database of billions of legal docu-
ments and records. She entered her password and then
left. Jim typed *Criminal History,* which took him to a
new menu. When prompted, he punched in *Long Beach*
and then *Mark Jackson.* The computer hummed and
conducted the search before returning over two
hundred matching results.

"Oh, boy. This is going to take a while." Jim settled
in for the long haul and began checking each record.
Three hours later, he exhaled a sigh of relief. Jim had
found *his* Mark Jackson. He scanned Mark's information
closer.

July 21, 1999, arrested for destruction of school property.
May 12, 2002, arrested for indecent exposure.

Jim chuckled to himself at such a disgusting
thought.

November 8, 2003, arrested for possession of marijuana
and drug paraphernalia.

Jim hit the "Print" button, satisfied with his efforts.
He then clicked into Microsoft Word and typed up a
professional-looking cover letter and cover fax for the
fictional company "Wolf Employment Screening."

Later that afternoon, Jim sipped coffee from a
styrofoam cup inside a small 1950s themed diner and
stared at the phone booth against the wall. He looked
nervous and guilty. He glanced down at the cover letter
and Mark's criminal record. Jim shook his head, unable
to go through with his plan. This wasn't how he
wanted to get a job. He stood up to leave when the
sign in the diner's window caught his attention—
"Help Wanted."

As if on cue, a listless waitress with lifeless eyes

passed by Jim's table. "More coffee before you head out?" The daily grind had taken its toll.

"No, thank you," Jim said. He couldn't help but think of Maggie. This was her future if he didn't do something. Out of all the men in the world, she chose him, and fetching coffee would be her reward. He grabbed the papers, stood, and marched into the phone booth. With new resolve, he picked up the receiver and dialed. He tapped his fingers against the side of the phone until the receptionist greeted him. "Banner & Brown, how may I direct your call?"

"Human Resources, please," Jim said with a fake Texas accent and a bad one at that.

A moment later, a female voice picked up, "This is Joan Thomas."

"Howdy, ma'am, my name is Gerald King. How are you today?"

"I'm fine. What is this about?"

Jim shifted his feet in the tiny phone booth. "Well, ma'am, I'm with Wolf Employment Screening. We do background checks on your employees."

"Wolf Employment Screening? We don't use that company?"

"That's odd. We were recently contracted by your firm—just three weeks ago. Perhaps that's why you haven't heard of us." Jim bit his lip, wondering if his ruse would work.

"I doubt it," Joan said.

"Well, why don't you check with your supervisor, but in the meantime, can I get your fax number? I have your first report here for an employee by the name of Mark Jackson."

Jim wrote the response down on a napkin. "Okay. Got it. Thank you, ma'am. This will come through in a few minutes."

Two days later, Jim stood in his small kitchen in front of the humming microwave in a pair of sweatpants from college. When the timer dinged, he pulled out two steaming Hot Pockets—gourmet dining at the Sloane residence.

The phone rang. Maggie answered it. "Hello?—Yes, he is. One moment." Maggie covered the speaker with her hand and whispered to Jim, "It's someone at Banner and Brown." She thrust the phone into Jim's hand.

"Hello," Jim said.

Robert's voice greeted him, "Jim, this is Robert Banner. How are you?"

"I'm good, and you?"

"I'm fine. Thank you for asking. Listen, I'll make this quick. A position has opened up. If you want it, it's yours. Be here tomorrow at 9:00 a.m."

"That's great. Yeah, 9:00 a.m. is perfect. Thank you."

Jim hung up and found Maggie smiling from ear-to-ear. She couldn't be more proud of Jim and jumped into his arms to give him a congratulatory hug. It was a good thing she couldn't see the guilty look on his face as he held her. Jim felt like he'd just sold his soul.

CHAPTER NINE

JIM'S EYES SNAPPED OPEN, AND HE FOUND HIMSELF sprawled out on the bathroom floor with his face pressed against the cold, hard tile. Morning light streaked in from the crack under the door.

Jim pulled himself to his feet and opened the door. He squinted as his eyes adjusted to the brightness and drifted over to the window. The snow had stopped. Jim pulled the printer and cushions away from his makeshift blockade and grabbed the pen holder from the ledge. He grimaced at the result—a half of a swig of water, which he gulped.

Jim moved to the toilet, unzipped his pants, and prepared to relieve himself. As he tried to get things started, he opened and closed his mouth, hoping to produce some saliva to ease the pasty cottonmouth that had set in. "What I wouldn't give for a drink of water," he muttered to himself.

A trickle of urine splashed against the porcelain bowl. The sound of liquid triggered an idea, albeit a revolting one. He stopped peeing, and with his pants still undone, hobbled out of the bathroom and over to the executive bar. He pulled out a clean glass and tucked it between his legs.

A small stream trickled into the cup. Upon finishing, Jim studied the glass—only about a quarter full. He swirled it around and took a faint whiff. The pungent odor made him cringe.

Jim closed his eyes and brought the glass to his lips when the phone rang. Almost thankful for the interruption, Jim's eyes flashed open, and he picked up the receiver.

"Yeah?"

The disguised voice mocked, "A vintage year for urine, is it?"

"Kiss my ass."

"Oh, how the mighty have fallen," the voice said.

As Jim listened, he caught a glimpse of himself in the bathroom mirror, holding a cup of urine with chapped lips, a pale complexion, sunken eyes, and rumpled clothes. The sight frightened him; he needed out.

"The big intimidating real estate executive who negotiates million-dollar deals over fine filets and Dom Perignon, and yet here you are about to drink your own piss. So sad. Well, bottoms up!"

Click.

Disgusted by his reflection and infuriated by the taunting, Jim hurled the glass against the mirror, shattering it and spilling piss all over the wall.

With nowhere else to direct his frustration, Jim paced the office and peered out the window. It was a cold and dreary day. Thousands of people lived in the city, and he couldn't reach one.

Far off in the distance, a faint staccato sound perked Jim's ears. *Chuff, Chuff, Chuff.* It was a helicopter. Jim scanned the skies until it came into view. He banged on the window and yelled, "Hey! Over here!"

When Jim realized the futility of his banging, he ran back into the bathroom and grabbed the largest shard of broken mirror.

The chopper cruised toward the building.

Jim rushed to the ventilation window and pulled his head and arms outside.

The chopper continued approaching.

Jim angled the mirror to reflect sunlight in the faint hope of signaling the pilot.

The helicopter was as close as it was going to get to the towers.

Jim fumbled with the mirror, but clouds masked most of the direct sunlight. "Come on. Come on!"

The chopper continued on its course and passed by.

Jim kept toying with the mirror, hoping to catch a break in the cloud system, but no such luck.

The phone rang.

Jim pulled himself back inside and answered it.

"Clouds are getting thick. Maybe you'll get lucky and get more than a few flakes of snow this time," the voice said.

"Don't worry about me, I'm fine."

"Really? How long since you last drank anything, hmm? And I don't mean alcohol or piss."

Jim clutched the phone like a vise, his anger growing.

"Do you have a tight feeling in your stomach yet? Dry mouth? A little light-headed, yes? Don't worry, Jim. That's normal. You can also expect headaches, dizziness, impairment of judgment."

Jim clenched his teeth.

"I wouldn't worry until you start dry heaving. Once the seizures start, then you've got real problems."

"Is that what you want to see?" Jim barked, his frustration boiling over.

"Perhaps."

"So looks like you're still sour over losing your job. Isn't that right, Mark?"

The voice laughed through the electronic filter. "I don't think so. Nice try, though."

"I mean, Eduardo," Jim tossed out.

"Are you going to guess all the people you've screwed over? I don't think you have that kind of time."

The comment silenced Jim.

"Tell me, Jim. Has it been worth it—all the people you've stepped on?"

"If I stepped on you, then yes."

"There's the fire I like to see. You'll be running this company in no time."

"Maybe, I will."

"You have to make it past Christmas first."

Click. The line disconnected.

Jim tossed the phone aside, then plopped down on the stripped couch cushions. His mind wandered as he tried to figure out the identity of his captor. Jim grabbed a legal pad and started writing clues. He scribbled *"Bad things happen to good people," "Ghost of Christmas*

Past," *"People I've screwed over,"* and one of the voice's last statements, *"There's the fire I like to see."*

That phrase paused him. Jim picked up the letter opener and resumed his activity from yesterday, scraping away at the wood paneling.

"There's the fire I like to see," Jim said aloud.

CHAPTER TEN

JIM'S THOUGHTS RETURNED TO HIS JOB INTERVIEW with Robert ten years ago.

"What I'm looking for is someone with fire and passion," Robert said.

Jim's memories shifted to yesterday's morning meeting. When Jim reacted to Sam's assessment to reject Montgomery Plaza, Robert said, "Something to add, Jim?"

Jim leaned forward in his chair. "Robert, our holdings have dropped fifteen percent over the last three years. We can't keep watching from the sidelines."

As Jim recounted the exchange, he rubbed his head, frustrated at himself. He had challenged Robert's leadership in front of all the other executives. How could he have been so arrogant and stupid?

Jim imagined Robert on the phone as he paced about his office, admiring the various plaques, newspaper clippings, and other assorted corporate memorabilia. "You'll be running this company in no time,"

Robert said through a phone with a high-end electronic filter.

"Maybe, I will."

"You have to make it past Christmas first."

Robert hung up and marched about the office. "No way some snot-nosed kid is getting the company I built from the ground up."

Jim held his head in his hands and smirked at his thought. "That makes sense. He's got more money than God, and he could just fire me."

As Jim rested on the couch, he shivered from the cold. He resumed chipping away at the wall to take his mind off the temperature, thirst, and hunger. After several minutes, he ran his fingers across the spot. A tiny hole had begun. "Thirty more years and I might tunnel through." He rubbed his head in frustration and then an idea froze him. Maybe someone already did the tunneling.

Jim stared up at the heating vent. Two Phillips head screws held the grating in place. He pulled a guest chair under the vent and stood on top of it. Using the side of the letter opener as a rudimentary screwdriver, Jim loosened the iron screws. Once he had them started, he finished the job by hand, and the grating fell and clanged against the floor. Jim inspected the exposed shaft. A tight squeeze.

Jim climbed on the back of the chair and balanced himself on its edge. He then hoisted himself up and wriggled his way into the shaft. Once in, he whipped out his zippo, flipped it on, and quipped with a perfect Bruce Willis delivery, "Come out to the coast, we'll have a few laughs."

He inched forward, his entire body now encased in the metallic tube. Another three feet and the duct turned ninety degrees to the left. Even a child would find squeezing around challenging, let alone a full-grown adult. Jim angled his body. With an inch to spare, he slugged the turn. After managing the feat, Jim paused for a rest. He searched for a little space to regroup, but there was none. Up ahead, the tunnel revealed only darkness.

With little choice, Jim continued worming himself forward. Ten more feet and Jim reached another corner, but he grew wearier and more claustrophobic with every second. Jim pressed on and summoned his energy to contort and wrangle his body into positions he never imagined were possible.

Midway through the maneuver, Jim paused. There was a strange noise up ahead.

Tick Tick Tick Psst Wooosh.

A blast of hot air engulfed Jim. The heater had kicked on.

Determined, Jim squirmed around the corner, but he couldn't move fast enough. His flailing only complicated matters as his left arm became wedged under his body.

The temperature climbed, and beads of sweat formed all over Jim's skin. He was cooking in what may as well have been a giant oven. Panic set in, and Jim's eyes filled with fear and frustration. He needed out.

He made the inevitable decision to begin a hasty retreat. With the temperature still rising and his exposed skin getting redder every second, Jim wrangled his arm free and pushed backward.

Little by little, he squirmed himself back until his toes touched the first corner. The turn presented a more daunting challenge feet first, but the threat from the intense heat caused Jim to push, pull, and bang his way through—anything to squeeze around. He turned the corner and inched back the last straightaway.

Mercifully, he felt his feet dangling over the much cooler office, but as he slid his body out, he scraped his ribs against a piece of jagged metal. Jim winced in pain, causing his foot to miss the back of the chair. He tumbled to the floor and rolled his left ankle. Exhausted, sweaty, and overheated, Jim writhed on the carpet in anguish.

As he caught his breath and held his foot, he checked the gash on his side. Just a shallow cut, but it hurt. He grabbed his tie off the floor and wiped the blood away. When he stood, his leg buckled from the shooting pain in his ankle. He sat down and used the tie to make a rudimentary wrap.

The phone rang.

Jim crawled over to the guest phone and picked it up.

The garbled voice laughed. "A little hot under the collar, eh Jim?"

"Don't quit your day job. Comedy isn't your thing, pal."

"Where on earth did you think you were going?"

"I don't know. It seemed like such a nice day to take a crawl through the ventilation system," Jim said.

The voice continued to laugh. "You have no idea where those vents lead. Neither do I for that matter, so we'll just leave the heat on to keep you out of the walls."

"Fine by me. It was getting chilly in here, anyway," Jim said, and then attempted to keep the conversation going. "So, why don't you give me another hint about who you are? All you've told me is you're the Ghost of Christmas Past."

Jim grabbed his pad of paper and prepared to take notes.

"Fair enough, why don't we look at the present."

Jim wrote, *"Ghost of Christmas Present?"*

"Don't you find it strange that you disappeared over the Christmas holiday and no one is looking for you? No one even cares."

"My wife and kids are expecting me. They'll find me."

"I wouldn't count on it. As we speak, your wife is probably sitting at home explaining to your two boys that daddy had an emergency at work that he had to take care of. A bedtime story I'm sure they've heard more than once."

The insult stung, in part because that scenario could be playing out right now. "Well, you seem to have me pegged. But how about you? Kinda pathetic that you'd spend your Christmas holiday tormenting someone as 'worthless' as me."

As Jim spoke, a revelation hit him. The guest phone had five other lines available, and his primary phone rested on his desk.

"No one said you're worthless, Jim. You're worth quite a bit now, aren't you?"

"Is this some sort of ransom? How much do you want?" Jim put the legal pad down and hobbled over to his desk, stretching the cord as far as it would go. He looked out the window, wondering if anyone was watching. Jim eyed the main phone with intrigue.

The voice chuckled. "You can't buy your way out this time, Jim. This isn't one of your little side deals."

Jim froze. How did this person know about that?

"Who the hell are you?"

"Have I finally got your attention?" the voice asked.

Jim gritted his teeth.

"Start talking about the deals, Jim. How do you get them?"

Jim's mind raced as he pieced together a new escape plan. He stared at the phone on his desk and then at the guest phone. "You want to know how I get them?"

"Yes, tell me."

"I'm always thinking two steps ahead." Jim flung the receiver back at the guest phone, and in a mock fit of frustration, shoved files and his phone off the desk. He limped about the office and discreetly kicked the phone across the floor.

Jim sat down on the couch, hidden behind the painting. He put his foot up, happy to take the weight off, and then placed the guest phone next to his desk phone. "Time to get out of here. Come on, call back, pal."

CHAPTER ELEVEN

AFTER HOURS OF WAITING, JIM'S ENTHUSIASM FOR HIS plan had turned to boredom. Beads of sweat formed on his forehead as the heater continued to raise the temperature. He stared at the legal pad, now covered with notes. *Who knew about his side deals?*

Jim tended to the scrape on his ribs while large sweat rings pooled in the underarms of Jim's t-shirt. He took it off and wrung it out, trying to squeeze droplets of perspiration into his mouth. The reward for his efforts—five salty drops. When was this guy going to call back?

Jim hung his head out the window to cool himself off, then sprawled out on the sofa, and did the only thing he could. He chipped away at the wood paneling and got lost in his thoughts. In his last conversation, the tormenter said, "Why don't we look at the present?"

"Who would be out to get me?" Jim asked out loud, and then chuckled. "Who wouldn't be?" He jammed the letter opener hard against the wall, causing the metal to give way and buckle. He tossed it aside and then picked up one of the wood chips. He studied it and remembered when he first saw the paneling four years ago.

EXPERT ARTISANS INSTALLED the wood as Jim watched with pleasure. Frank approached from behind, where two other workers positioned the massive oak doors.

"That's a nice choice, Jim."

Jim turned to Frank. "It's Brazilian cherry wood. Between that and the Italian leather sofas, it's nicer than my house."

Frank chortled and elbowed Jim in the side. "Maybe you should just move in here?"

"It wouldn't be the first time I spent the night, something my wife never gets tired of reminding me of."

Both men chuckled, but Frank stopped the frivolity. "Kidding aside, she should know that we appreciate all your hard work."

"Thanks and I've been meaning to tell you I appreciate you giving me your office," Jim said.

Frank patted Jim on the back. "You earned it, and it isn't like I'm downgrading by taking a corner office."

"True. But I gotta be honest, I feel a little guilty."

"Why's that?" Frank asked.

"We're spending all this money on my office, and the raises for the secretaries were smaller than last year, plus there's Sam..." Jim glanced out the doors at Sam toiling away.

Frank stepped in to block his view. "Jim, you're

thinking about it all wrong. You pay for their salaries. Each deal you bring in gives them a job to come to every day. I know Sam's been here longer than you, and yet, you've gotten a few more... perks than he has, but let's be honest. He's a nice guy, but he's cut from a different cloth. We count on you for things that Sam could never do."

Jim nodded and shook off his guilty feelings.

"Your co-workers may not like it when they see you getting things like this, but your job is to go after bigger and better deals. If you're going to sell clients, they need to see what you've earned and what you're about." Frank waved his hands at the opulent office, transforming before their eyes. "You need to look the part 24/7, which is why I have one other thing for you."

Frank tossed Jim a set of keys. "Porsche Carrera. It's parked in the garage."

Jim stared at the keys in his hand, stunned. He couldn't stop a giant smile from spreading across his face.

Through the doorway, Sam glanced over from behind his desk. There were two worlds right now—Jim's plush world and everyone else's.

As Jim's thoughts drifted to Sam, he noticed the Montgomery Plaza files strewn about the floor. He then glanced at his legal pad and focused on the note that read, "*How does he know about the side deals?*"

Jim imagined the future, and Sam working at his desk, which was now in Jim's office.

Robert poked his head in. "Sam, magnificent job on the Montgomery deal. I appreciate you stepping up in the wake of Jim's tragedy. Come down to my office later and let's talk about your future with the company."

Sam grinned, ear-to-ear, as Robert exited.

Jim snapped out of his haze and shook his head. "You don't have it in you, Sam."

Not sure of anything anymore, Jim sat with his back against the arm of the couch, staring at nothing in particular. He was lost not in thought but in emptiness; his body and mind in neutral.

His gaze fell on the massive doors with their hand-crafted designs etched into the wood and the thick brass handles.

Jim rose to his feet, hobbled over to his desk, picked up his printer, and carried it to the door despite his injured ankle. He raised it over his head and launched it against the handles. The entire front of the machine smashed against the rigid metal. Jim lifted it again and hurled it even harder. Pieces splintered off. Jim grabbed the largest chunk and flung it against his barrier to freedom. Circuit boards, rollers, and gears littered the floor.

The printer was now destroyed, but Jim's fury raged on. He heaved up the computer monitor and chucked it against the door. "Open, dammit!"

The screen cracked as it struck the handles. Jim paused his tirade long enough to tug on the handles.

Still no headway.

Getting back to business, the monitor soon met the fate of the printer as Jim repeatedly bashed it against the handles. He pulled at them a second time.

They were starting to give.

Inebriated with the idea of escape, Jim pummeled the handles with anything not nailed down, his violent energy building to an explosive crescendo. First, the fax machine, then the computer CPU, and then a chair. Jim raised the heavy wooden chair high for a mighty strike and thrust it down. Like a beaten boxer, the battered handles yielded and fell to the floor.

Exhausted, Jim laughed to himself. "I did it. I did it." He called out, "You couldn't beat me."

Jim tossed the chair aside and nudged at the splintered hole left by the handles. It was stuck. Jim pushed with more force, but the doors didn't budge. This wasn't possible. Jim had broken the handles. He should be free, but he wasn't.

The sound of Jim pounding on the door and his whimpers of despair echoed throughout the bullpen. "No! I don't deserve this."

The office fell silent.

On the verge of tears, Jim sat with his back against the door. Options and time were running out.

Jim's lips were chapped and his mouth dry and sticky. His skin, aside from a pale color, now had several cuts and scrapes from the vent and splintered office equipment. This beaten man was a far cry from the energetic business executive from a few days ago.

As he sat on the floor, the framed picture of his wife and two boys, one of the few items left on his desk, haunted him.

Maybe he did deserve this.

CHAPTER TWELVE

SIX YEARS AGO, A VERY PREGNANT MAGGIE straightened up the apartment. She centered a dark green ceramic vase filled with fresh red roses on the kitchen table, which was nothing more than a card table with four folding chairs around it.

The phone rang, and Maggie answered, "Hello."

"Did you get them?" Jim asked from his first office at Banner & Brown. Spartan compared to his current lavish set up, this windowless space contained an IKEA desk and stacks of boxes.

Maggie smelled the flowers. "Yes. They're gorgeous, but we don't have the money for things like this."

"We will." Jim eyed the files strewn across his desk.

"How's work?" Maggie asked.

"Busy. How are you feeling?"

"Fat." Maggie rubbed her belly.

"Fat and beautiful," Jim said.

"Yeah, right. I'll be losing about eight pounds in the next week, so don't go trading me in just yet."

"I wouldn't dream of it."

Robert knocked on Jim's door.

Jim switched back to work mode. "I gotta go. I'll talk to you later." *Click.*

"Okay, love you," Maggie said, but Jim was already gone.

Robert stepped in the doorway. "Hey Jim. How's the Flemish land deal coming?"

"Uh... great." Jim patted a thick file. "I got everything ready."

"Good. We have a meeting with the sellers at 5:00."

"Five today. Great. No problem," Jim said, but panic swirled in his stomach. He wasn't close to being ready. Robert left, and Jim slumped back in his chair. He glanced at his watch—six hours until the deadline. Jim took a deep breath and psyched himself up. He could do this. He opened the file and got to work.

Two hours in and the phone rang. Jim ignored it and kept working, digesting every detail he could about the property. A half-hour later, the phone rang again. Jim pressed on. At least three more dockets needed review. By the second one, he found time to scarf down a bag of Doritos. The phone rang a third time. He eyed it, then let it go to voicemail.

When Jim's final report finished printing, he glanced at the clock—4:15. He'd done it, and with time to spare. Jim grabbed his phone and dialed his voicemail as Robert popped in.

"It's go time. All set?" Robert asked.

"Sure. One minute," Jim said.

Robert nodded and left.

Jim listened to the first message. "Hey Jim, it's

Maggie. I, uh, think it's starting. Please call me when you can. I got a taxi to the hospital just in case. Bye."

Jim's heart raced as the second message played. "I'm at the hospital. The doctor's not sure if this is it or not. Please call me, though."

Jim pressed the prompt for the third message. "Jim, they said it's probably going to be a few hours. Please call me. I need you. Love you. Bye."

Jim hung up and debated his next move.

Robert called out from down the hallway. "Let's go, Jim."

Jim checked his watch and considered his options. Maggie said it would be a few hours. He could make this work. Jim grabbed his report and left for the meeting.

———

THREE HOURS LATER, Jim arrived at Pennsylvania Hospital. He dashed through the entrance, asked reception for the right floor, then took an elevator ride, and hurried down the hall. Jim searched the rooms until he found Maggie asleep on her side.

A nurse came up from behind and instructed him to go to security to check-in, but Jim ignored her. He pulled up a chair beside the bed and rubbed Maggie's shoulder. She stirred and awoke with tired eyes. A warm smile spread across her face upon seeing Jim by her bedside. "Jim!"

"Hey beautiful," he said, stroking her hair.

"Where were you? Did you get my messages?"

Jim paused before answering. "I've been in meetings

all day." He kissed her forehead. "They went great, Maggie. Afterward, Robert hinted I might get the promotion—"

"We have a son," Maggie said.

"What?"

Maggie nodded. Jim was a father. The realization sank in, along with the guilt that he wasn't there for the moment. Jim smiled and hugged Maggie.

"I'm sorry. I'm so sorry I missed it."

As JIM RELIVED THE MEMORY, a solitary tear streaked down his cheek. "I should have been there."

Frustrated at his inability to do anything constructive, Jim snatched the picture of the Banner Towers and smashed it against the desk. Other wall hangings soon followed, along with books, papers, and other assorted office supplies. Jim had lost it. He seized the Christmas tree and hurled it across the office.

"Ten years. Gone. I missed my son's birth, missed Little League, missed holidays, birthdays, anniversaries." He flung a box of paper clips against the door, which sent them flying in every direction. "Eighty hour work weeks, for what? So, I can die in my office? I can make things right. I earned better than this. I deserve better than this!"

Jim grabbed a picture and prepared to heave it against the wall, but paused when he saw it was the picture of his wife and kids. He surveyed the office and what he'd done. The office was ransacked.

Breathing hard and covered in sweat, Jim slumped

down at the foot of the couch. Any energy he had left was spent.

He pulled his sock down and checked his ankle. Swollen like a balloon, it also had disgusting shades of purple and red streaking across the skin.

The phone rang.

Jim snapped back to survival mode. He had one last chance.

CHAPTER THIRTEEN

JIM'S HEART RACED AS THE PHONE RANG A SECOND time. He studied the two phones side by side and cautiously answered the desk phone. This was it—his last and best chance to escape. "Hello?"

"That was quite a display. You haven't given up, have you?"

"No, just needed a little exercise." Jim hit the mute button, picked up the guest phone, and hit a second line, praying for a dial tone. Bingo. The monotonous buzzing was music to Jim's ears.

"You need to save your energy for something a little more productive. Are you ready to start talking?"

Jim put the receiver of the guest phone against his chest to muffle the sound of the dial tone. He depressed the mute button on the other phone. "First, answer my question."

"What's that, Jimbo?"

"Why me?" Jim asked before hitting mute again and dialing 9-1-1 on the guest phone.

"Why you? Think about all the people you've hurt."

Jim put the receiver aside and unmuted himself. "Sounds like you're bitter because you can't cut it in the business world." He hit mute again and grabbed the other phone. It was ringing!

"Maybe I should cut the same corners you did. It's time to come clean, Jim."

"Come on. Answer dammit." Jim cradled the second phone against his leg and depressed the mute button. "What corners have I cut?" Jim muted it again. The guest line continued to ring.

"Where are you getting the money for the bribes and kickbacks?"

Jim fell silent. How much did this person know?

"Are you there?" the voice asked.

A faint voice from the guest phone interrupted Jim's daze. "9-1-1, what's your emergency?"

He raised the guest phone to his ear, but forgot to mute the other line. "Thank God! I'm trapped in the Banner Towers..."

"Clever boy," the voice said.

Click.

Both lines were cut.

"Hello? Hello?" Jim tapped the other line, trying to get a dial tone. Silence. Dejected, he held his head in his hands. "It's OK. They still have to do a follow-up," Jim said, trying to convince himself.

Hours later, twilight settled in and Jim still prayed for a miracle. He assumed the authorities would at least have to check in with security. Jim stared at the phone. "Come on, Keith. Get your ass up here."

Jim dropped his head between his legs, rubbed his

eyes, and imagined Keith sitting at his desk with his feet on the table, eating a bag of chips, when the phone rang. He picked it up. "Banner Towers, Security Guard Keith Campanero speaking." Keith listened to the caller before responding, "No, everything's quiet. Probably a crank call. I'll check all the offices and verify. Thanks for the call." He hung up and smirked.

Delusional, Jim shook his head. "The whole world is against me. Even Keith. Met him one day, and now he wants me dead."

Jim giggled. His situation somehow became comical as it became more dire. The voice kept playing in his mind, like a medley of clues. *Think about all the people you've hurt. Where are you getting the money for the kickbacks and bribes?*

Jim grabbed the legal pad and scribbled, *"SEC Inquiry"* followed by *"Sting Operation."*

Jim remembered meeting Keith for the first time two days ago. "You the new guard?"

"Yes, sir. Keith Campanero's the name. Started on Monday."

Was it a coincidence that Keith started right before this whole ordeal? Jim looked out the window at the opposite tower. "Who the hell are you, Keith?"

Jim imagined an undecorated office in the western high-rise filled with SEC investigators and computers. One agent surveyed Jim's office through a pair of binoculars, then keyed a radio. "Keith, we gotta get a confession out of him soon. He's in bad shape right now, and I think he's figuring it out."

From the security office of the eastern tower, Keith

sat behind the control panel. "He was going to figure it out, eventually. Trust me, he's about to break."

Jim shook his head at the lunacy of his delusion. "I've lost it." His pale face showed not only the lack of food and water but also the emotional wear and tear from the torment. "I'm going to die in my office."

He snickered at the thought. Dying in your office isn't the way most people imagine leaving this world. A little choked up, Jim cleared his throat. But something wasn't right. An unsettled look crept across his face.

Without warning, Jim bolted to the bathroom. He lifted the toilet bowl lid and keeled over. His stomach convulsed, but nothing came out. After several dry heaves, he slumped down on the porcelain tiles and collected himself.

He was in awful shape, and it was only getting worse. Jim lumbered back to the couch on his injured foot and collapsed. His fatigued soul gave in to sleep, but it wasn't a deep sleep. He shivered as his body reacted involuntarily to the lack of fluids. The shaking triggered a coughing fit that caused Jim to spit up blood on the carpet. Unable to do anything and too tired to care, Jim kept trying to slip into a sound slumber.

As he drifted in and out of consciousness, the shadows in the office seemed to come alive. The oak doors cracked open, and a shaft of light shot across the floor. Jim's eyes widened as Keith entered.

Through parched lips, Jim croaked, "Keith."

Keith didn't respond, and Jim remained on the couch, too weak to move. Eduardo appeared behind Keith with his cleaning supplies in hand.

"Let me know when you're finished, so I can lock up," Keith said.

Eduardo picked up several files strewn across the floor.

"Eduardo?" Jim muttered in a hoarse voice.

Eduardo continued to clean with no response. Sharon and Sam stepped through the doorway.

"It's a shame, isn't it?" Sam asked.

Sharon nodded half-heartedly. "Yeah, a real shame."

Robert walked into the office, escorting Maggie. She held a handkerchief, and had puffy, red eyes.

"Maggie!" Jim perked up.

Maggie didn't respond as Jim reached out an arm for her.

"Please take whatever you'd like. I'll have Eduardo box it up for you," Robert said.

A tear rolled down Maggie's cheek as she scanned the office. Jim looked on with confused eyes. Why couldn't she see him? Finally, she declared, "There's nothing here that I want."

And with that, Maggie turned and left.

"Maggie! I'm right here. What are you doing? Don't go." Jim shouted in despair and desperation.

Robert followed Maggie out of the office. Sharon, Sam, and Eduardo left behind them. Keith was last one to depart as the phone rang.

"What's wrong with you people? I'm right here!" Jim said.

Keith locked the doors behind him.

"I'm sorry. Please. I'm sorry," Jim bellowed.

Brrriing. Brrriing. Brrriing.

Jim blinked and awoke to morning sunlight streaking through the window and the sound of the ringing phone.

Brrriing. Brrriing. Brrriing.

His vision was nothing more than a bad dream. He crawled off the couch and grabbed the phone off the floor. "Hello?"

The mysterious voice greeted him, "Merry Christmas, Jim."

Too weak to engage in a verbal battle, Jim hung up. He dragged himself to his feet and hobbled into the bathroom. Through the reflection of one of the shattered pieces of mirror, Jim found dried blood on the edges of his lips. Forgetting his situation, he turned the faucet on to wash it off. Of course, no water came out.

Jim meandered back into the office. His foot landed on something that cracked. He glanced down and saw the picture of his wife and two children, now smashed. Jim knelt down and pulled out the photo from the broken glass. He hobbled over to his desk and searched the remnants on the floor until he found the macaroni picture frame his son had made. He slid the photo inside even though it didn't quite fit and then set it on his desk.

Jim leaned back in his executive chair and admired his family. He'd give anything to be with them today. Maggie's angelic face smiled at him. She was so beautiful. How did he get so lucky?

"You should have chosen someone else. I never deserved you in the first place. You should have chosen—"

Jim's words triggered something. His brain kicked into overdrive as he tried to piece the puzzle together.

One name fell from his lips, "Charlie."

CHAPTER FOURTEEN

JIM REMEMBERED MEETING CHARLIE TWO DAYS AGO IN the back alley and asking for a favor.

Charlie responded, "No such thing as a small favor with you, Jimbo."

Jimbo—the stupid nickname Jim hated, and one that the voice also used. Maybe it was a coincidence, but maybe not.

When Jim tried to persuade him to help with the Montgomery deal, Charlie asked about Maggie. Jim mentioned Maggie left him, and followed up with the wisecrack, "Who knows, maybe you'll get another crack at her."

He made that biting comment to get Charlie acting with his emotions, which was good for the deal, but it was only effective because there was some truth behind it. Jim rubbed his head and forced himself to re-live the uncomfortable moment when he first learned that fact.

Seven years ago, Banner & Brown held its holiday schmooze fest at the Four Seasons hotel for all of its employees, clients, and business associates. It was a high-class affair, even though many of the guests used the open bar at the event to enjoy more than their fair share of wine, spirits, and special holiday punch.

Jim was busy yakking it up with Howard Malloy, a prospective client with old money. "So, it's settled. I'll have my office call your assistant, and we'll set a tee time," Jim said.

"Winner gets the building, right?"

Jim offered his best courtesy chuckle. "From what I've heard about your golf game, we'll leave the business until after we're done. Now, if you'll excuse me, I'm going to find where my wife ran off to."

Jim snaked his way through the crowd, searching for Maggie. He passed by Frank.

"How did it go with Old Man Howard?" Frank asked.

"Piece of cake," Jim said.

Frank laughed and elbowed Jim. "Don't tell Robert how easy it was—you'll make me look bad."

"I almost feel bad doing it to him," Jim said, and he meant it.

Frank laughed louder. "You got a good sense of humor, Jim. I knew I could count on you."

Jim played along and snickered as if he was joking before moving on. He spotted a much younger Sam with more hair, standing alone and looking very uncomfortable.

"Hey Sam, quite a shindig, huh?"

Sam perked up, happy to be talking with anyone. "Oh, yeah. Really nice."

"Have you seen Maggie?" Jim asked.

"I think I saw her talking with Charlie somewhere in the lobby. You want me to show you?"

"No, thanks, big guy." Jim patted Sam on the shoulder and then made his way to the hotel lobby. Maggie was nowhere to be found. He scanned the area until he spotted her outside with Charlie. By the dramatic hand gestures and Charlie's furrowed brow, it was obvious the conversation was anything but typical holiday mingling.

Jim slipped out a side door and stood behind a pillar so he could listen without being seen.

"Why now, Charlie? And how can you say that when you and Jim are—"

Charlie interrupted, "Friends. We're friends, Maggie. But that doesn't change how I feel. Before you and him, there was us."

"One night does not equal an 'us,'" Maggie said.

There was an uncomfortable pause.

"Why didn't you tell me this then?" Maggie asked.

"Because I was with Christine. Remember?"

"And now, I'm with Jim."

"Can you tell me you don't think about it?" Charlie asked.

Maggie didn't respond.

"Just because the timing hasn't been right doesn't mean we're not right."

"I can't, Charlie."

"Why not?"

"Because I'm pregnant."

Jim almost fell backward. This was the first he'd heard of the pregnancy.

"And because I love Jim." Maggie hurried back inside.

Jim considered confronting Charlie or chasing after Maggie, but the shock from the revelations left him leaning against the pillar for support.

As Jim replayed the memory in his office, he clenched both fists, furious he'd been beaten and didn't see it coming. His imagination and paranoia, now in overdrive, created the conclusion to the story.

Charlie would arrive and knock on Maggie's front door. She'd open it and look stunning, like she always did.

"I'm afraid I have some bad news about Jim," Charlie would say with fake empathy.

Maggie would fight back the tears and grab hold of Charlie for support. He'd embrace her with both arms and a small grin would spread across his face. Victory was his.

Jim couldn't stop his mind from creating the denouement to his depressing tale. The next Christmas, Charlie, Maggie, and the two boys would pose for the annual photo. His sons would cling to Charlie like a father.

Jim's frustration boiled over. This ending to the story of his life needed to be stopped. He looked for something to break, but everything in the office had already been destroyed.

Brimming with rage, Jim racked his brain for some way out, something he hadn't yet thought of. Edgy and impatient, he kept returning to the smashed picture of the Banner Towers.

He focused on his building—the majestic eastern

high-rise that would become his tomb, unless he could figure a way out. With death so close at hand, his mind was free to consider more extreme possibilities. Jim zeroed in on the fiftieth story—the top floor. The rooftop and its stairwell were right above him. Fed by a new sense of hope, his body found nourishment from his old resolve.

One last chance for survival.

Jim limped over to the window and pressed his face against the glass, but was unable to see the corner of the building.

He slid his head through the ventilation window, and the icy breeze blasted against his cheeks.

Fifty feet to his left, Jim saw the corner, a large circular pillar that jutted out, making it impossible to get around. But above it, the masonry protruded and lipped underneath.

Jim looked down. Death. He yanked himself inside, his hate replaced by the sickening sensation he experienced from being on the ledge before. "No way! There's gotta be another way." His logical side came to the rescue. "Come on, Jim. Pull it together. It's not like you've got a lot of options here."

The picture of his family resting on his desk called to him. There were no other options left. If he wanted to see his wife and boys again, Jim had to do the impossible.

Jim took one last look at the now seemingly comfy confines of his office before turning his attention to the window. He slipped the tie off his ankle, stuck it in his pocket, and then slid outside for the final time.

CHAPTER FIFTEEN

JIM TWISTED HIS BODY SIDEWAYS TO AVOID extending too much of his weight over the edge.

Once on the ledge, the cold air chilled him to the bone. Nothing separated him from an eternal rest except twelve inches of concrete, his balance, and control of his fear.

Jim stood up and leaned back against the glass. He side-stepped little-by-little towards the corner.

Midway into his journey, his hand grazed the first pillar that signaled the end of his office and the start of Robert's. Jim extended his injured leg around and searched for a footing. Upon finding it, he shifted his weight and slid to the other side. He completed the maneuver, which, unfortunately for Jim, was the simple part.

His teeth began chattering as he inched forward along the ledge. Just twenty-five more feet to the corner, although under the circumstances, it seemed like twenty-five miles.

After several more side-steps, Jim felt the heavenly touch of cold concrete—the corner pillar.

Above his head and several feet out from his hands, the curled masonry teased him. Close enough as an option, but far enough to be a high risk proposition.

Jim reached out, but it wasn't close. He grabbed the bloodied tie from his pocket and held one side in each hand. Jim flung the tie up and out, hoping to catch the slack on the lip. His efforts fell three inches short. He leaned forward and tried again. Closer, but no cigar. Jim leaned even further and attempted a third time. The tie glanced off, and Jim lost his balance. He was going to fall. Jim flailed his arms and swung his torso backward until he steadied himself.

Gun-shy and frustrated, Jim couldn't get the tie around the curl like this. "Come on, cut me a little slack here!" He half-chuckled at his poor choice of words. He looked down at the world far below and wrestled with the inevitable decision he must make. "You gotta be kidding me."

Do or die. Jim summoned all his courage for one last attempt. He wrapped the small end of the tie around his left hand and the thick end around his right. He snapped the thin cloth to make sure his grip was secure. With an intense focus, Jim gazed up at the curled concrete.

After a deep breath and a quiet prayer, Jim raised the tie above his head. He leaned his weight forward until he hit the point of no return. He was on the verge of falling.

Jim pushed off with his feet and jumped towards the concrete lip. In midair, he snapped the tie forward. Just as the falling sensation set in, the tie caught the lip, which abruptly halted Jim's fall. Dangling like a fish on a hook, Jim swayed, and the tie shifted back and forth, inching dangerously close to the curl's edge.

Jim waited for the swinging to subside, but the stitching on the tie started to tear. His eyes bulged, and he glanced down. Bad idea. Nausea settled into the pit of his stomach as he stared death in the face. Jim looked up at the tie, the only thing separating him from becoming a meat waffle. The cloth ripped further. He struggled to pull himself up with what little strength he had remaining. Just as the tie tore completely, he swiped for the concrete masonry and grabbed hold. The ripped fabric fluttered toward the ground.

After a deep breath, Jim hoisted himself above the edge of the roof. As his head peered over, the intrusion startled a small flock of resting pigeons. Wings and feathers flapped above and to the side of Jim's face, terrifying him and causing his arms to buckle.

Jim fell back under the ledge, his arms on the verge of permanent muscle fatigue. He struggled and pulled his head higher, but found nothing to grab. Instead, he discovered a forty-five-degree concrete slope about twelve feet wide and a six-inch wrought iron railing running around the inside perimeter.

Jim swung his good leg over the ledge. With nothing to grip, he clawed at the concrete, which tore at Jim's fingers, but he fought on, every millimeter a tiny victory.

Jim grunted his torso up and rotated his lower half around the corner until his entire body pressed against the ledge. If even a finger slipped, the consequence would be immediate and deadly. Plastered against the concrete, he scraped himself up, inch-by-inch. He was almost there. His toes dangled over a seven-hundred-foot drop, and an iron post, a little over an arm's length in front of his face, dared him to reach for it. The metal rod was part of fencing that ran around the building—a safety perimeter designed to keep people on the inside of the rooftop, a place Jim desperately wanted to be. His tired eyes pleaded for mercy. Just a few more inches and he'd be safe. Finally, he'd be safe.

Jim pulled his feet over the edge, but his footing was about to give. With his last ounce of strength, he lurched for the iron post, but his hand missed, and he slid backward toward the drop. His arms flailed for anything to stop the descent, but there was nothing. A look of pure terror spread across his face.

As death approached, his life didn't flash before his eyes. Instead, his mind filled with millions of micro-thoughts, with the last being Maggie and his two boys.

He clamped down onto the concrete surface and stopped his fall just as his feet slipped back over the edge. Fueled with an iron determination, his fingers clawed their way back.

Jim pulled himself up the incline, with sweat dripping from his brow. He lunged up the final few inches and grabbed the iron post. Clinging to it by his fingertips, he tried to muster the strength to get over this last obstacle, but his grip gave out.

Out of nowhere, a gloved hand reached over the bar and locked onto his wrist.

Jim stared up in disbelief. "You?"

CHAPTER SIXTEEN

JIM AFFIXED HIS GAZE AT THE GLOVED HAND HOLDING his wrist. His life was literally in this person's hands. Would they let go? Then, with one quick thrust, Jim was yanked up onto the roof. Jim collapsed to his knees as Keith hovered above.

"Keith, thank God! You got my message? Have you called the police?"

Keith didn't respond. As Jim struggled to get to his feet, Keith appeared on alert. He was more like a grizzly bear than the giant teddy bear Jim remembered.

Keith held out his hand for Jim to stay on the ground. "Just relax, Jim."

A horrifying realization overwhelmed Jim. "You're not here to help me, are you?" Jim's stomach sank. "And you're not with the SEC."

Keith remained silent.

The puzzle came together in Jim's mind. "There's no way you're working alone. Who hired you?"

"That's between my employer and me," Keith said.

Jim kept thinking out loud, driven to know who did this to him. "Charlie couldn't hire you."

Jim's thoughts drifted back to the holiday party seven years ago when he passed by Frank. *"Don't tell Robert how easy it was—you'll make me look bad."*

Jim recalled what Frank said when his office was furnished four years earlier. *"Your co-workers may not like it when they see you getting things like this..."*

Jim slouched on the rooftop and grimaced in frustration. "I can't believe I didn't see it. So, does Frank have the balls to face me, or is he going to have you do all his dirty work?"

The door to the rooftop swung open.

"Merry Christmas, Jim." Frank emerged from the doorway and approached. "It's good to see you. Those phone conversations were far too impersonal."

"I should've seen it sooner. It burns you that I can do things for this company that you've only dreamed about. It always has."

"I like to think I've had a hand in the company's success too, Jim. Unfortunately, all our success has attracted the attention of certain regulatory agencies," Frank said.

"The SEC inquiry? You want to know how I pulled off the deals so you can turn me in?"

"I'm the CFO, Jim. I'm responsible for all the financial transactions of this company. If someone is going to go down for that, it's not going to be me."

"So I'm the fall guy?"

Frank snorted. "That's one way to put it."

"Overworked executive with a guilty conscience and

his marriage on the rocks jumps to his death, huh?" Jim asked.

Frank shrugged.

Jim's eyes narrowed. He lunged at Frank, but Keith moved in and subdued him. Jim rammed his elbow into Keith as hard as possible, which had no effect. Keith flung Jim to the ground with enough force to daze him. There was no more fight left. Keith was much too powerful, and Jim had already given all he had. He rolled over to his knees and coughed up blood.

"It's over, Jim," Frank said.

"I've given my life to this company!"

"Not yet, you haven't. But I'd like to make you a final offer." Frank stepped casually in front of Jim. "Sign a confession detailing everything you've done and take full responsibility."

Jim scoffed. "Just give you a nice tidy suicide note, so there are no loose ends?"

"Well, there is one other option. If you and I were to both implicate Robert—"

"Robert gave you your start, you disloyal son of a bitch," Jim snapped.

"I was afraid you'd feel that way." Frank motioned to Keith, who grabbed Jim and dragged him toward the edge of the roof.

Frank stepped forward and caught Jim's arm. "One last chance, Jim."

Jim shrugged out of Frank's grasp, punched Keith, and dashed to the door. But it was locked. He rammed it with his shoulder in a feeble attempt to break through. Frank and Keith watched Jim flail against the door with zero worry he'd escape. Jim was trapped.

A helicopter emerged in the distance and approached the rooftop. Jim flapped his arms hysterically to catch the pilot's attention. The chopper flew closer, kicking up wind in all directions. Frank and Keith shielded their eyes as it set down on the helipad just above them. Jim ran up a small staircase towards the chopper as the door opened and Robert stepped out.

Jim was both relieved and confused. "They were going to kill me, and Frank has been—"

"Relax, Jim," Robert said.

Frank and Keith strolled up the stairs as the helicopter shut down, and the blades slowed. It soon became quiet, almost peaceful on the rooftop.

Robert approached Jim and held up his hand for Keith to stop. "At ease."

Keith took a step back as Robert handed Jim a bottled water from his pocket. "You need this."

Jim stood speechless, trying to put it all together. He twisted the cap and chugged the water.

"You want to drink that slowly," Robert said.

"But I don't—"

"Your confusion is understandable," Robert said.

"You couldn't have known... I don't...," Jim stammered.

Robert smiled at Jim. "I know what you've been through, the mental and physical torment. You're as low as you're ever going to be, and yet you never sold us out."

The reality of Robert's involvement sank in. Fatigue and shock caused Jim's legs to give way. He dropped to his knees.

"This was never about Frank trying to steal the company or you pushing Frank aside," Robert explained.

Frank nodded in agreement.

"I've spent my life building Banner & Brown, Jim. I've gone through three wives, never had time for kids, and lost a lot of friends along the way. This company is my legacy, and I need to know who I can trust to protect it."

Jim couldn't stop tears from filling his eyes. "This was all some sort of test?"

"And you passed," Frank chimed in.

Frank and Robert smiled at each other.

"Drink a little more, Jim. You need it," Robert said.

Jim sipped the water. It tasted so good.

"You see, Jim, to truly know who you can rely on, you've got to break a man down until he's got nothing left."

Jim's mind finally put it all together. This went all the way back to his interview with Robert, when Jim tried to impress him with how much he knew about him. *"You served two tours in Vietnam and spent four months in a POW camp before coming home and starting Banner Real Estate."*

"The four longest months of my life. Made the business world look like child's play."

Jim pulled himself to his feet, still in total disbelief.

"I learned everything I needed to know about myself in those four months as a POW, and I've learned everything I need to know about you in these four days. You'd be shocked by how many guys I watched sell out their country to save themselves a little pain. I imagine it would take a lot less to sell out your company."

"But I could've died," Jim said.

"We never wanted to lose you, Jim. We didn't bargain on you going out the window." Robert pointed at Jim as if he should feel guilty over what he'd put them through. "You had us pretty worried."

"Robert didn't believe me when I called and told him. We never thought you could climb up to the damn roof!" Frank chortled at both Jim's bravado and stupidity.

"I always said this kid had balls the size of Texas." Robert patted Jim on the back. "And through all the physical and mental torture, you were never willing to sell us out."

"You're both insane." Jim shook his head. "You can't seriously think you'll get away with this. What's to stop me from going to the cops?"

Robert and Frank both laughed.

"I'd love to be there when you tell them that two upstanding corporate executives locked you in your office," Frank said.

"The office will be cleaned up, Jim. There won't be any evidence." Robert shook his head to emphasize his point.

"There's a lot I can prove. I'm sure the SEC will be all ears," Jim said.

"Careful, now," Frank said. "Every questionable transaction will lead right back to you. You'd just be turning yourself in."

Robert patted Jim on the back a second time and beamed like a proud father. "Besides, there's no need for any of that now. We know what you're made of, and quite honestly, you far exceeded even our expectations. You always have."

Jim replayed his career in his head. He remembered the moment when he chose work over Maggie when she was pregnant.

Jim pulled up his voicemail and heard Maggie's pleading voice. "Hey Jim, it's Maggie. I, uh, think it's starting. Please call me when you can..."

Outside Jim's office, Robert walked down the hallway, where Frank waited.

"His wife's called him like twenty times," Frank said.

"Jim's a team player," Robert replied.

Frank smirked. "Yeah, he'll have other kids."

Jim struggled to exit his office under the weight of the files.

Back on the rooftop, Robert explained, "I told you that your efforts on the company's behalf don't go unnoticed. They've never gone unnoticed."

Jim swallowed hard as the realization swept over him like a tsunami. So many important events in his life weren't because of him. Robert and Frank were always there, pulling the strings. The holiday party seven years jumped to mind.

Jim drifted through the crowd after speaking with Howard Malloy. He passed Frank.

"How did it go with Old Man Howard?" Frank asked.

"Piece of cake," Jim said.

Frank chuckled. "Don't tell Robert how easy it was—you'll make me look bad."

"I almost feel bad doing it to him," Jim said.

Frank laughed louder. "You got a good sense of humor, Jim. I knew I could count on you."

Jim played along and snickered as if he was joking. He moved on to find Maggie while Frank walked over to Robert at the other end of the bar.

"Jim's doing well."

Robert sipped a gin and tonic. "Good. Keep him motivated."

"What are you thinking? A raise? Women?" Frank asked.

Robert considered the options.

"No, he wants to be like us. Give him an assigned parking spot, a personal secretary, and let's move him into the office."

Frank nodded, knowing what that meant.

On the rooftop, Robert pointed at a stunned Jim. "I had a feeling about you from the very start."

Ten years ago, Frank, with less gray hair, met with Robert.

"Look at this." Robert handed Frank the fax from Wolf Employment Screening that Jim sent.

"What is it?" Frank asked.

"Mark Jackson's criminal record."

"That's not surprising. That guy is a louse. He's more interested in avoiding work than finding creative ways to grow the business."

"It's not even the background agency we use." Robert showed Frank the cover sheet.

"Is this a real agency? Looks like a high school kid made this."

Robert leaned back in his chair and handed Jim's resume to Frank. "Or a recent college grad."

Frank inspected the two faxes. "Same fax number. Guess someone really wants the job."

"You can't teach that kind of tenacity," Robert said.

Frank nodded. "I'll bring him in."

Jim continued to process everything about his life

and career, but his confusion remained. "So you proved you can trust me, now what?"

"Now, we talk about your promotion," Frank said.

Jim perked up. "Senior VP?"

Robert cackled. "I wouldn't go to this trouble for a Senior VP title, Jim. I'm talking about the big one."

Jim shook his head. "I don't understand."

"I'm getting old, Jim. I can't run this company forever."

"You mean...?" Jim couldn't even say the words.

"I want you to take over my legacy, Jim. I want you to be the next CEO."

Jim's head spun. He'd gone from the absolute depths to the top in mere minutes.

"This ordeal may seem extreme," Robert said. "But it isn't when you understand that this company is like my child. I have to know that the person I leave in charge is going to fight for it like I would."

"What about Frank?" Jim asked.

"I'm a numbers guy, Jim. We need a visionary at the helm. I told you before that everyone's paychecks depend on you, and that includes me."

Jim couldn't even wrap his mind around it all. "CEO?"

"Everything you always wanted, Jim," Frank said.

"Money, power, perks." Robert motioned to the chopper. "The private helicopter, company jet, corporate houses."

Robert and Frank pressed all the right buttons. With every word, Jim forgot his outrage and imagined the possibilities.

"You'll answer to no one. It'll be your company.

Banner, Brown, and Sloane. You'll be...," Robert looked around with a wry smile and concluded, "At the top."

Robert extended his hand to shake and seal the deal. Jim hesitated and soaked up the surreal moment. His eyes settled on the helicopter. That was now his, along with so many other things. He turned to Robert, who gleamed with pride. Jim couldn't help but feel a tremendous sense of accomplishment. He stepped forward and accepted the handshake.

"Your hand is freezing," Robert said. "Let's get you inside to celebrate." Robert led Frank and Jim as Keith stayed behind on the roof.

Robert headed towards his office, but Jim paused at the doors of his own, where two steel door jams sat wedged between the floor and the outside handles. It was a simple mechanism—the type of device purchased at the local hardware store for a few bucks. Jim tossed them aside, incredulous that small metal rods kept him imprisoned and in misery. He pulled the door open and stepped inside his office. The image startled Jim. The ransacked room looked like a war zone. Jim drifted to the window and stared at the western high-rise, deep in thought. Banner & Brown owned that building, too. How easy must it have been for Frank to watch him? A pair of cheap binoculars would do the trick.

As Jim mused, he didn't notice Robert and Frank approach from behind. "Don't worry, that will all be cleaned up by tomorrow," Robert said.

"I just need to grab a couple things." Jim searched the office until his gaze fell upon the picture of his family in the macaroni frame. He picked it up.

"It's natural to feel sentimental after what you've been through. It'll pass," Robert said.

The small stack of files on Montgomery Plaza rested near Jim's feet. He put the picture down and scooped up the files.

"I've got a lot of catching up to do. I lost several days of work over this."

Robert guffawed and turned to Frank. "I told you he was the one. Let's get a drink in my office."

Robert smacked Jim on the back, who wore the same expression as when he first sold his soul many years ago.

CHAPTER SEVENTEEN

THE SUN ROSE OVER THE PHILADELPHIA SKYLINE, AND the city awoke from its holiday slumber.

Inside Banner & Brown, the bullpen sprang to life as everyone shook off the long weekend. Phones rang, secretaries rushed to answer them, and papers flew. It was just as it had been before the extended break, except for the energy. The anxiety and stress that existed before Christmas was gone.

Eduardo watered the plants as he grooved to music on a brand new iPhone and headphones. Sam sported a top of the line suit and chatted with Sharon, who wore a gigantic smile. Even William, the intern, had an extra bounce in his step as he distributed the mail.

Robert waltzed in on cloud nine, his legacy now safe. He greeted his employees as he passed, stopping only to glance into Jim's office, which was completely repaired and restored to its original condition. His face dampened on finding it empty.

He moved on to his own office, where Frank waited.

"He's not here yet," Frank said.

"Everyone else seems in high spirits," Robert said.

"Yeah, go figure. When we cut the Christmas bonuses, I thought it was going to be a glum mood around here for a while."

"I hated doing it, but these are lean times, and we had to pay for Keith and all the repairs," Robert said.

"What if he changed his mind?" Frank asked.

"You worry too much, Frank. He'll come back."

"How can you be so sure?"

Robert eyed Frank. "You did."

An email notification popped up on Robert's computer. The message was from Jim. Robert froze as he read the subject line—*My Resignation*. He clicked it open, and his jaw dropped. The email had been sent to everyone in the office. Robert surveyed the bullpen and noticed the staff glued to their screens, or looking over the shoulder of a colleague to read.

It is with genuine sadness that I am announcing my resignation from Banner & Brown. I know many of you won't share my sentiment since I haven't always been a good friend or even a good co-worker.

Sharon held her hand to her mouth in shock and surprise. Sam shook his head in disbelief as he skimmed the email.

There is no way I can make it up to you, and for that, I am sincerely sorry. All I can do is offer an explanation. I thought I had life all figured out. I clawed my way to the top and found myself with an incredible job, cars, houses, and piles of money. But as is often the case in life, the higher you climb, the further you can fall. For me, the fall came on Christmas Day. That's when I realized that for all my apparent success, I was a failure. I had defined myself by the salary I earned, the title I carried, and the office I worked in.

But it was never enough. There was always someone with more, and I thought that if I became that "someone" I'd be happy. For all that I didn't have, I took for granted everything that I did. I've been told you learn a lot about yourself when you have nothing. What I learned is that I gave up the one thing I wanted more than anything and now, I'll give everything to get it back.

Robert sat at his desk with his head in his hands, still trying to process Jim's resignation. Everything seemed like it had all gone according to plan. He racked his brain and searched for answers. His mind drifted to the last thing Jim said to him.

———————

Two days ago, Robert, Frank, and Jim headed to Robert's office for a celebratory drink. The ordeal was over, and Robert's successor had been declared. Everything was perfect. Robert reached into his desk drawer and produced Jim's cell phone. "Guess you'll need this back." He tossed it over.

Jim caught it and read the display. Fifteen missed calls from Maggie.

Robert poured everyone a shot of brandy and raised his glass for a toast. "To the future."

Frank followed Robert's lead and held up his cup before turning to Jim, who looked at the two men like he was seeing a ghost—a ghost of Christmas future.

"To the future," Jim said in a hollow voice, and then put the glass down. "My stomach isn't quite ready for alcohol. You know, I really should get going. My family's probably worried sick. I'm sure you're dying to get home to your families, too."

Robert's and Frank's faces read like an open book—not really.

"Maggie will understand when she sees your new pay stub," Frank joked.

"And you can always upgrade," Robert added.

Frank snickered, and Jim forced a fake chuckle before standing up. "I'm taking the company helicopter to the airport." It wasn't a request.

"Of course. Just one of the many perks you'll enjoy. I'll get a ride with Frank," Robert said.

Jim passed by his office on his way out. He stopped and looked at the wreck inside. The one thing that stood out was the picture of his family resting on the desk. He walked in and grabbed it. Jim then scooped up the Montgomery files off the floor and found the company address list amidst the clutter before rushing out.

Jim darted back up the stairs to the rooftop, where the helicopter and pilot waited.

"Airport—I want to make the two o'clock flight," Jim said.

The pilot nodded and fired up the propellers. "We've got plenty of time."

"Good, I need to run a few errands first." Jim buckled into his seat and then studied the address list.

Minutes later, there was a knock on the beat-up door of a tiny apartment. Eduardo opened it in thick winter pajamas. He looked around and wondered who had knocked, but no one was there. He stepped outside and his foot kicked an envelope sitting beside a small box with a bow. The envelope read, *"Christmas Bonus."* Inside, he discovered a pile of hundred-dollar bills. He opened the box and found a brand new iPhone. A smile spread across Eduardo's face.

A few blocks away, William, the intern, walked outside his parents' upper middle class home and noticed an envelope on the ground with his name on it. He tore it open and removed a concise note. *Let's have that career talk. There's a lot I need to tell you. Hopefully, you won't make the same mistakes I did. Best, Jim Sloane.*

Jim entered the receiving area of a massive apartment complex. He scanned the mailboxes until he found the one marked 210. Jim pulled out the keys to his Porsche and a card that read, *"This car shouldn't give you any trouble, and I hope you made it in time to surprise your mom for Christmas. Best, Jim."*

Jim dropped both in the mailbox and then rushed out of the complex. He crossed the street into a small park where the helicopter waited. He hopped in and signaled for the pilot to take her up.

In a well maintained home in the middle of suburbia, Sam, his wife and two kids gathered around the Christmas tree and opened their presents. A knock at the door interrupted the festivities. Sam stood and answered the door. He found the Montgomery Plaza files at his feet. There was a Post-it note on top where Jim had scrawled, *"You earned these. I know you'll do the right thing."*

In the sky above, the helicopter flew on to its final destination.

A few hours and a quick plane ride later, Jim stood outside the doorway of Maggie's house, holding a bouquet of lilies. He had cleaned himself up as best he could, but he still looked like hell, and butterflies filled his stomach. Maggie had no reason to take him back.

IN THE OFFICE BULLPEN, employees of Banner & Brown whispered and gossiped after finishing the email. They'd gotten a glimpse of what life was like at the "top." A few peeked up from their desks into Robert's office.

Robert clenched his fist and stared at Frank. "We need to get him back." The phone rang. "I don't care how far you have to go or what you have to do." The phone kept ringing. Annoyed, he picked it up. "What is it?"

"Merry Christmas, Robert," Jim said.

"You're making a mistake, Jim. Just come back and we'll forget all about this."

"I just called to make sure we're clear on one thing. If you ever get any ideas about coming after me, there's a nice present ready to go to the FBI and SEC. Your legacy and your name will be ruined forever."

Robert gritted his teeth. He'd been check mated.

"Think about your career, Jim. Are you really going to be happy with some run-of-the-mill job in the sticks?"

A long silence followed. Robert waited, wide-eyed. Maybe he'd gotten through to Jim.

Cleaned and refreshed, Jim sat in Maggie's kitchen on the phone, while Maggie helped get one of their sons ready for practice in the living room. "Jim, are you ready to take Matt to practice?"

Jim lowered the receiver. "Be there in a sec." He raised it back to his ear and smiled. "Absolutely."

"Jim, wait—"

Click.

Jim was gone—for good. Robert paused for a moment and then turned his back to Frank. He looked out at the view from his fiftieth floor. Even this magnificent view no longer moved Robert. Nothing did. A hint of a smile crept across his face. The kid got out.

Jim placed the phone in the cradle and headed out to the living room, where his son waited. The two walked to the front door and passed by the mantle above the fireplace where the pictures from all the Sloane family Christmases were displayed.

As the years passed, the photos increased and the Christmases of the future became the Christmases of the past. Jim's and Maggie's smiles got bigger in each picture as they grew older together, and their two boys became young men.

Everyone looked happy, especially Jim, who had his life back.

We hope you enjoyed *High Risk*. If you did, please consider leaving a review on the site where you acquired the book. Reviews are tremendously helpful, and we love receiving feedback from readers! If you're interested in checking out our other books, please visit https://www.maynardmcnally.com.

Thanks for reading, and thank you for your support!

www.ingramcontent.com/pod-product-compliance
Lightning Source LLC
Chambersburg PA
CBHW050739230626
47052CB00003BA/535